CHRISTMAS JOY

However, each man among you [without exception] is to love his wife as his very own self [with behavior worthy of respect and esteem, always seeking the best for her with an attitude of loving-kindness], and the wife [must see to it] that she respects and delights in her husband [that she notices him and prefers him and treats him with loving concern, treasuring him, honoring him, and holding him dear].
Ephesians 5:33 AMP

Taiwo Iredele Odubiyi

PRAISES FOR THE BOOKS OF
TAIWO IREDELE ODUBIYI

I am reaching out to express my gratitude for the profound influence your books have had on my life. Growing up, reading your works was not only a source of inspiration but also a foundation in shaping my character. Your stories guided me toward values and virtues that have helped me grow into a woman committed to living with purpose, integrity, and faith. Your unique ability to convey Christian virtues in a relatable way truly resonated with me as a child and left a lasting impact on my journey. I often find myself returning to those lessons, drawing from the wisdom and grace you imparted through your writing. Thank you for allowing God to work through you and for being a blessing to so many, including myself. I would like to order copies for my girls … as many as you have written, ma. May the Lord continue to bless you in your writing and ministry, reaching new generations with the same grace and truth that has touched my life. With heartfelt appreciation.   -
Aderonke Faseru

In 2008, while I was in secondary school, I came across *Love Fever* on my desk, and since then, I've become an avid reader of your books. I own every single one, except for the ones yet to be published! 😄 Your writings have truly blessed me, and I've received great feedback from people to whom I've gifted your books. Thank you so much for helping me gain a deeper understanding of the scriptures through your work. I am so grateful to have come across your books, ma. - *Adenike Kazeem, Lagos*

I want to express my heartfelt gratitude to you for directing me to the place where I could find your books. I was able to buy just 14, and I've already read two of them. I hope they restock soon so I can buy another set ... I must say, I've been truly blessed by your writing. Your words have ministered to me in a profound way, and I'm so grateful that you allowed God to use you as a vessel. Thank you again for your obedience to share your gift with the world. I'm looking forward to reading the rest of the books. God bless you, ma.
- *Ijiwole Kehinde Oluwakemi*

I started reading your novels at age 12. Actually, my dad bought one as a birthday gift for my elder sister. (Till date, I still don't get where he got the nice idea from: that your books are actually the best among the rest 🌟). I started with *This time around.* I was always too lazy to read but to my surprise, I didn't want it to end 😩 . You are so wonderful, Momma, and you shall forever remain my one and only author 🖤 . Your books are the only novels I ever want to keep seeing. I no longer know how to read any other novel; I'm addicted *fa* . We have been on your case, since *aye tipetipe* . - *Classy Magrel*

Same here! The first book I read was *Oh Baby* back in SS1 in 2009. I shared it with my sister, and we both got hooked! If I come across another one of your books now—chai, it'll be another Joy Overflow! The way your books continue into another is pure joy; the connection flows seamlessly. I remember *Marriage on Fire* is a continuation of another book, but I've forgotten the title. - *Abiodun Oderemi*

Your books have been a tremendous blessing to me. I started reading them back in my secondary school days when my sister's friend introduced me to them. I remember reading *Love on the Pulpit, Tears on My Pillow, This Time Around,* and *Love Fever.* From that moment, I fell in love with your books, but I couldn't find them again until 2019, during one of the toughest seasons of my life. My heart longed for your books, so I reached out to you on Facebook, and you directed me to a bookshop. I got four books, read them, and my soul was uplifted. Your books aren't just stories—they are powerful messages from the Father. Greater Grace, Mommy . - *Bunmi Akereja*

ACKNOWLEDGMENTS

I thank You, Lord God, the I AM, my Rescuer and Lord, For:

Yet another book. *Thank You for the great privilege and grace that You have given me to speak and write for You, and about You: about Your will, Your ways, Your word, and Your wondrous love. Thank You for the mercy You have shown me in allowing me to know You,*

All the wonderful family members You have blessed me with – *for all that they do, and for always being there for me,*

This book's editor, Babatope Olabode. You're a familiar name on my acknowledgment page, and for good reason. Thank you for always being available to edit my books, for your thoroughness, and for your unwavering commitment to this ministry.

Families, friends, fans, and my avid readers - those who have been with me since the beginning of this great journey, and those who joined along the way, reading my books, supporting, praying, and encouraging me,

Lord, let those who read this book experience Your touch, transformation, and blessings, that they may know You are the real Author and that Your love and mercy truly endure forever!

It's All About You!   **Taiwo Iredele Odubiyi**

EXCERPTS

… "Your closet is already overflowing with clothes, bags, and shoes in every style imaginable, for every occasion. If I check them, I'm sure I'll find some still with tags on." His voice was sharp.

"It's not like I buy the same things."

Lolu's brow creased, and his mouth hung open in disbelief as he stared at her, as if he couldn't believe she had just uttered those words. …

… Adesua chuckled. "I'm sure he means well. But let me ask you … do you love your husband?"

"Do I love him?" Moyo thought for a moment. "Yes, I do."

"But ... are you *in love* with him?"

Moyo raised eyebrows. "Didn't I just answer that? Or is this different from the first question?"

Adesua nodded. …

… Without a word, she reached out and took his hand in hers, squeezing it gently.

He looked at her, surprised. "What's this about?"

She shook her head, and then said, "Thank you."

"For what?" He asked, puzzled.

"For being you." She replied softly, resting her head on his shoulder.

DEDICATION

To God

&

To married men who, through patience, prayer, and
purpose, overcame, or are overcoming life's challenges.

# CHAPTER 1

THAT FRIDAY EVENING, thirty-four-year-old Moyo sat in the living room of the three-bedroom apartment she lived in with her husband, Lolu, and their two-and-a-half-year-old son, Jeremiah, fondly called Jerry.

On her way home from work, Moyo, who worked at a law firm, had picked up her son, Jerry, from the preschool he attended. Normally, Lolu, her husband, handled this since he was a teacher in a High School and closed at 4pm. Lolu also worked as a photographer on the side, and today, he had an event to cover. With him unavailable, Moyo had to step in. Thankfully, she had no meeting scheduled and was able to leave the office on time.

After picking up Jerry at 6pm, she stopped at a restaurant to get him some food, which he was now eating. Jerry was seated on his small blue plastic chair while his food and a cup of water were on his plastic table of the same color. As he ate, he watched a cartoon playing on the medium-sized flat-screen TV in the living room.

Having eaten before leaving the office at 5.30pm, Moyo, who was dark in complexion, slim, and of an average height, now sipped on a cup of *gari* while using her phone. She had mixed the processed cassava flakes with cold water, milk, and sugar.

When she heard the front door unlocking, she knew her husband had arrived. Glancing at the clock, she noted it was 9.02pm. *Let's see how much he brings home today*; she thought with a sigh.

Soon, the door opened, and a tired-looking Lolu stepped into the living room, his black camera bag slung over one shoulder. He was tall and dark in complexion.

Moyo didn't bother to get up as she glanced at him and greeted coolly, "Welcome."

But Jerry sprang up from his chair and ran toward him with an excited shout, "Daddy! Daddy!"

Lolu smiled faintly and dropped the bag onto the nearest side table before scooping Jerry up into his arms. "How are you?"

"I'm fine!" Jerry replied cheerfully, his small arms wrapped around Lolu's neck.

"Good boy." Lolu said, putting him back down. "Now, go and finish your food, okay?"

Jerry nodded and scurried back to his seat, his focus returning to the food on his plate.

"How has your day been?" Lolu asked Moyo, his voice weary.

"It's been good."

He sank into the single sofa across from Moyo and sighed. "Ahh."

"How was your outing?" She forced herself to ask.

"It went well." He said and rubbed a hand over his face.

He had spent the day at the High School where he taught Social Studies, and when he closed at 4pm, he had gone home to grab his camera bag. Afterward, he left for the event he was scheduled to cover, and now, he was very tired.

He spoke again. "As I mentioned in the morning, I didn't charge the woman much since she's a church member. What she paid isn't significant." The woman had hired him as the photographer for her modest fiftieth birthday celebration which held in the large compound of her house.

Moyo's lips pressed into a thin line as she looked at him. *Same story as usual. For how long will this continue?!*

"I'm starving. What's there to eat?" Lolu asked.

"Well, there's not much at home." She answered. "We have some cooked beans in the fridge. Want me to warm it up for you?"

"Beans?!" He repeated, frowning. "Why beans? I had that last night. Besides, you know I'm not a big fan of beans."

You can't be serious, Moyo thought, though she said calmly, "Well, as you can see, I'm drinking *gari*." She had chosen to drink *gari* as a subtle way to prove to him that there wasn't much food in the house and he needed to put more money down for groceries.

"Is there nothing else?" Lolu pressed.

"There are some bread rolls in the fridge."

Lolu's frown deepened. "You know I don't really like those. Why isn't there any solid food?"

"Because there's no solid money!" She shot back.

"No solid money? To cook food?" He stared at her as if he didn't think he'd heard her well.

"No!" She responded firmly. "How much do you actually put down for groceries?!"

The statement made him angry. "How much do I—?"

She cut him off. "It's not much! I've told you I need money to buy groceries!"

"And I told you I was going out today and would get some money! How could you say there's no money to cook? Don't you have some money you can use to buy food until I give you more?"

No, I won't keep doing that, she thought. "I don't have any money." She said flatly.

He stared at her again for some seconds, clearly not believing her, before finally asking, "So what am I supposed to eat?"

"You can manage the beans or the bread. We also have noodles; that won't take long to cook. Or," she added pointedly, "You could bring from the money you were paid so I can buy food for both of us from the eatery down the street, that is if it's still open."

Without a word, Lolu pulled an envelope from his shirt pocket and tossed it onto the table. "You can suit yourself." He said in anger.

Grabbing his camera bag, he stood up, and as he headed toward the bedroom he shared with Moyo, she called after him, "What would you want me to buy for you?"

"You don't need to go out. Give me whatever I can eat right away, please." He muttered, not bothering to turn around.

Moyo shrugged. *You brought this upon yourself*, she thought.

But just as he opened the bedroom door, she remembered that the gown and a pair of shoes she had bought earlier in the day were still on their bed.

Oh my God! She exclaimed under her breath. She had completely forgotten to put them away. Another argument was bound to happen before they went to sleep tonight; she was certain of it. Lolu would see the items and would complain.

Just last week, they had an argument because she bought a gown.

"It's my money." She had told him when he complained.

"You need to stop saying, 'It's my money.'"

Why should I stop saying that?! Moyo thought, almost scoffing to herself. *I won't, but I'll keep reminding you that I work hard for my money, so I have the right to spend it as I choose, until you finally understand. I won't let you tell me how to spend my money.*

In addition to her salary from the law firm, she took on side jobs as a lawyer, which earned her a significant income.

He went on. "Even if it's your money, that doesn't mean you should buy everything you see or spend it recklessly. You're married with a child; we have bills to pay!"

"And you're also married with a child!" She retorted swiftly. "You're the head of this home; the husband, the father. Maybe if you had a better job, my spending wouldn't be such an issue."

"It would sooner or later become an issue even if I earned a million, because this isn't how to manage money, especially as a Christian. What we have is still enough. Plenty of people have less and still make do." He had responded.

"Well, that may be true, but I don't want to live that way. I earn a good salary and should be able to buy the things I want. This was how I lived before I married you. I dressed well and you must have married me because of that. I'm not going to start wearing rubbish because I married you!" She had pointed her right index finger at him.

She went on, her voice now trembling. "I know what I went through growing up. I won't allow you to take me back!"

Here we come again. "When will you stop talking about your past and see that I'm not your father? I've told you that things will improve with time."

"When?" She had asked, sounding frustrated.

"God will do it." He'd replied.

"Please, just get a well-paying job." She had whispered back then, her heart heavy with disappointment.

He took a deep breath, sensing her frustration. "We've gone over this so many times. You know quite well that I took the teaching job because I couldn't find a better one, not because I wanted a job where I'd close early and come home to sleep. And now I've added photography to make ends meet. I'm not lazy, Moyo. The least I expect from you is some encouragement." He said quietly.

She scoffed. *Encourage you? I won't!*

Lolu spoke again, "Don't worry. I will make it, with time. I'm praying; the Lord will help me."

With that, Moyo kept quiet. It wasn't worth arguing further.

Snapping back to the present, she braced herself for another argument; certain the same conversation would unfold all over again this evening, very soon.

How much did he bring home tonight anyway? She reached for the envelope on the table, opened it, and counted the money inside; it wasn't much. She let out a hiss of frustration and tossed the envelope back onto the table, her annoyance clear.

She thought back to the time shortly before their wedding when Lolu had suggested they open a joint account. Back then, he was earning a decent salary. She had refused however, saying it wasn't necessary.

Now, she was grateful she hadn't agreed.

****

When Lolu stepped into the bedroom, his eyes landed on two shopping bags lying on the king-size bed he shared with Moyo.

"It's a lie!" He muttered in disbelief. *Shopping bags again*? After all the conversations they'd had about saving money, had she really just bought more clothes?

Placing his camera bag on the floor, he checked the bags. One contained a new gown and the other had a pair of shoes. The purchase receipts were inside the bags, and pulling them out, his suspicions were confirmed—the items had been purchased today.

Today? That hit him like a slap. Didn't she just say she didn't have money for food?

Anger building, he marched back into the living room.

When Moyo saw him, she knew that the moment for the argument had come, and she returned her focus to her phone.

"When did you buy the stuff on the bed?" He asked, his voice tense.

Moyo remained silent, refusing to meet his gaze.

"Moyo?" He pressed, his patience wearing thin.

When she still didn't respond, he added sarcastically, "Oh, so now you've suddenly gone mute? You bought them today, didn't you?"

With a sigh, she put her phone down, looked at him, and answered in a defensive tone, "Look, I bought them because I need them."

"What happened to all the shoes and clothes you already have?" Lolu demanded.

Moyo folded her arms across her chest and looked away.

"Your closet is already overflowing with clothes, bags, and shoes in every style imaginable, for every occasion. If I check them, I'm sure I'll find some still with tags on." His voice was sharp.

"It's not like I buy the same things."

Lolu's brow creased, and his mouth hung open in disbelief as he stared at her, as if he couldn't believe she had just uttered those words.

He finally said, "Oh, okay, so you have money for more clothes and shoes … and bags and jewelries, but you don't have money to cook a decent meal for your family, right?"

Moyo rolled her eyes. "Let's be honest, Lolu. I use my money to cook sometimes, but today, I don't have that kind of money."

As they argued, Jerry looked at them.

"I see." Lolu said coldly, staring at her for a few seconds before turning and heading back to the bedroom.

Moyo hissed, equally upset.

Lolu entered the room and closed the door behind him, a little louder than was necessary.

Hungry, and angry, he stripped off his clothes and stepped into the adjoining bathroom for a quick shower, but the cool water did little to wash away the frustration he felt.

Why does Moyo behave this way?!

****

Unbothered by the tension that had just unfolded, Moyo picked up her phone and returned her mother's call. Her mother had called earlier when she was on her way home, but she hadn't been able to answer at the time. She suspected her mother called to remind her about the phone handset she had mentioned she needed.

The sixty-year-old woman, a widow, shared a close bond with her four children and made it a habit to call them regularly. Moyo was the eldest of the four, and she looked just like her mother, although taller. The woman had always made time for her family and business, but now that she was a Christian and her children were grown, she dedicated much of her time to her service to God.

Moyo and her three siblings considered their mother a good role model for them, and they were proud of her just as she was proud of them.

Raising them had not been easy for their mother however. With no financial support from her late husband, she had to juggle a business alongside her regular office job to cover their tuition and meet household needs. Determined to see them succeed, she also hired lesson teachers to ensure they performed well academically. Her sacrifices and efforts paid off as she had well balanced children. They excelled in their studies and later pursued careers they loved. Her first child,

Moyo, became a lawyer, her two sons became engineers, and her youngest child, a female, became an accountant.

Whenever the woman reflected on her children, gratitude filled her heart. She thanked God for His mercy, knowing that their smooth journey was not because she was a perfect mother but because of His grace.

She was also relieved that their financial struggles had not left lasting scars, at least none that she could see. None of her children had fallen into bad company, battled addictions, or faced legal troubles. She knew that Moyo was more affected by the financial struggles than her siblings, but she believed Moyo had overcome her fears. This, too, she counted as God's goodness in their lives.

"I missed your call." Moyo said after greeting her mother. "Is everything okay?"

"Yes. I just called to say hello." Her mother said warmly.

"Oh, okay. Thank you, Mom. Well, I haven't forgotten what I promised you. I'll take care of it soon." Moyo replied, already thinking about how to keep that promise.

"No problem, I understand. You don't need to worry about it if it's not convenient. I can still manage the one I'm using." Her mother reassured her. "I know that your husband is not earning much at the moment, and I don't want you to feel stretched."

"It's fine. I'll do it." Moyo insisted.

While Moyo spoke, her eyes wandered around the tastefully decorated living room. Lolu had rented the apartment about six months before they met, sharing it with a friend to split the rent, but when he and Moyo decided to get married, his friend moved out. In preparation for their wedding, Lolu repainted the walls, upgraded his queen-sized bed to a king-sized one, and purchased the black L-shaped sectional sofa she now sat on. The sofa was placed along one side of the light gray room, adorned with four multicolored throw pillows. The set included a single sofa and two movable storage ottomans, one of which now supported her feet.

The single sofa was positioned on another side of the room, near a round black wooden center table with two side panels. On this table sat a wooden vase, the TV remote, and one of Jerry's picture books. The gray-and-black patterned rug complemented the light gray curtains, and by the large window was a wooden chair and table where Lolu often edited photos on his laptop. In one corner, a small toy storage bin held Jerry's toys and his folding floor bed.

Six framed photographs adorned the wall: two from their wedding, one of the three of them as a family, two of Jerry, and one of Moyo and Jerry taken by Lolu himself. The room also featured an oval mirror which enhanced its spacious feel. Only Jerry's scattered building blocks introduced a bit of chaos to the otherwise orderly space.

Moyo continued her phone conversation with her mother, reassuring her that she would keep her promise soon.

"Thank you. But -" her mother's tone changed slightly, becoming more cautious. "As much as possible, discuss these things with your husband before doing them for me."

"Why, Mom?" Moyo asked. *Why do I need to tell my husband before doing things for my mother?* She had wanted to add but knowing that Lolu would be able to hear her side of the conversation from the bedroom, she didn't.

"Because you're married." Her mother answered anyway. "It's important that you and your husband are transparent with each other. Marriage is about sharing, Moyo … sharing the small things, sharing details, sharing plans. Some people don't realize that the small things can make a difference. The small things that people overlook usually build up."

Moyo's mother who became a Christian about six years ago, was now a deaconess in her church, and often shared advice like this. Moyo however didn't always want to hear it, especially now.

She sighed inwardly, feeling a bit of the weight of her mother's words but not entirely in the mood for such conversations.

"It's better to keep him involved; that way, you'll both stay on the same page." Her mother explained. "Sharing your plans with him might even encourage him to help or find a way to support you."

Moyo rolled her eyes and made a sound as she thought - how could Lolu support her when he didn't even have a good job?!

It was as if her mother read her mind when she spoke again, "It's not only money he can use to support you. He can support you by handling the situation for you."

She was about to respond to her mother's advice when Lolu entered the living room, now dressed in a black T-shirt and jeans shorts.

"Okay, Mom. I've heard. How are you doing?" Moyo asked, keeping her tone casual.

"I'm doing well; the Lord is good." Her mother replied.

"Okay, I'll talk to you later. I need to get food for my husband." She said, watching Lolu from the corner of her eye.

When her mother heard that, she quickly encouraged Moyo to go and attend to her husband and ended the call.

"Will you eat beans?" Moyo asked Lolu, hoping to smooth things a little.

He merely shrugged, indifferent. "I already said I'll eat whatever's available." He said curtly, the frown still lingering.

With a sigh, Moyo stood up and headed to the kitchen.

Lolu walked over to the refrigerator, opened it, and grabbed a bottle of water. He returned to sit on the single sofa, his expression still clouded by anger.

A few minutes later, Moyo returned, carrying a tray on which were a bowl of beans, a bowl of *gari*, sugar container, cutleries, and a bottle of cold water. She placed the tray in front of him, quietly hoping the simple meal might ease the tension between them, even if just a little.

When Lolu noticed the single piece of meat on his beans, he frowned and asked, "No more meat?"

"No."

He let out a sharp hiss, said a brief prayer, and began to eat without another word.

Moyo gathered the bowls and cutlery she and Jerry had used and took them to the kitchen to wash. Once she was done, she returned to the living room, picked up her phone, and headed to the bedroom to put away the shopping bags she had left on the bed earlier.

On a side of the bedroom wall were two framed photos— hers and Lolu's, alongside a wall clock. Opposite their bed, a flat-screen TV was mounted. On another side of the wall, near the door leading to their adjoining bathroom, stood a spacious walk-in closet which was thoughtfully divided in the middle, ensuring each of them had their own organized space for clothing and other personal items.

About twenty minutes later, she returned to the living room. Lolu was now in the kitchen, washing the dishes he had used while their son remained in front of the TV, still absorbed in his cartoon.

CHAPTER 2

LOLU SOON FINISHED in the kitchen and without a word, walked past Moyo, and straight into the bedroom, with the tension between them still hanging in the air, unresolved.

The way she spent money without consideration for his opinion upset him, but her seeming indifference upset him more.

And he was still upset because she hadn't apologized. She hardly apologized. She didn't even think she was wrong in any way or that something was not right in their marriage!

The money he made wasn't much compared to hers, but he gave everything to her. And whenever she spent money on the family, she requested a refund, and he always complied. What else did she want him to do? And how many husbands did she think would do that?

He sat on the edge of their bed with his elbows resting on his knees, his head bowed, and his hands clasped. Feeling frustrated and exhausted, and wondering where things had started to go wrong, he thought back to when they first met.

Back then, he had a good job, had this rented apartment, a car, and some money in his savings account. These might seem like small accomplishments to some people, but they were his.

He wasn't born again at the time, but he had a church he sometimes attended, and which he considered his church.

Before he rented the apartment and found the church, he lived with his parents. His parents were also not born again at the time, but they were committed members of an orthodox church and had brought him and his siblings up to know that God was real. Lolu went to the church with his family but stopped when he was in the University. His parents were not happy about this development, and when he graduated and returned home to live with them, they regularly encouraged him to go to church. They asked him to find a church he liked if he didn't want to attend their own church. After a while, he began to consider returning to church. He promised his parents that he would, but he never did until he rented this apartment.

He was going out one day when he noticed the church—*The Transformation Chapel*—which was about ten minutes drive from his apartment. He didn't know anything about the church but as he looked at the picture of the pastor and his wife on the billboard in front of the church, something tugged at his heart, and he decided to attend their service soon.

Two Sundays after, he was ready to attend the church's service. Dressing up, he left home in his car, and arrived at the church almost two hours late, just the way he planned it.

When he told his mother later that day that he was in a church in the morning, she was happy. His sister who was born again and attended a Pentecostal church wanted to know the name of the church, and when he told her the name, she said it was a good church. She encouraged him to keep going and give his life to Jesus.

He didn't return to the church until three weeks after, however. He told his parents that he was in the church again, and when he assured them that he would be there whenever he could, they were pleased. He was also pleased; now, his parents would leave him alone. Few days after, his sister's pastor visited his parents, preached to them, and they gave their lives to Jesus.

On Lolu's third time in the church in his neighborhood, he could see that the pastor was a true man of God, and he told himself that going to church once in a while to hear the pastor preach wouldn't hurt him.

That was how he began to claim to be a member of the church even though he didn't attend midweek services. He only showed up on Sundays, and sometimes not even then, yet he was quick to tell anyone who asked him that he was a Christian. He believed that what he did was enough, and he made sure to steer clear of any church activities, programs, or commitments. He also kept his distance from the pastor and the more serious members of the congregation.

He met Moyo through a friend, and she claimed to be a Christian too. When they started seeing each other, she told him that she didn't want sex before marriage as she knew it was a sin before God. Lolu respected her stance at first, but over time, a little pressure from him changed her mind.

He loved her and loved the fact that she was a lawyer, earned a good salary, and owned a nice car. In his past relationships, he had been the one providing financial support, but he reasoned that if he married Moyo, she would also be able to contribute to the household expenses.

And so, he decided to marry her, but as they spent more time together, he began to notice some things that unsettled him. The two major ones were their frequent arguments, and her attitude toward money. She saw his money as their money while her money was her money. Period.

He knew that these were red flags, but he chose to overlook them for three reasons. One, he thought if they got married, things would improve; marriage would make their relationship better. Two, he earned a good salary, and he didn't think her attitude about money could affect him much. Thirdly, he was ready to get married anyway. He was his parents' first child, and almost thirty two years old. None of his siblings was married yet, and his parents were eagerly anticipating a wedding. He decided not to delay wedding plans any longer.

When he introduced Moyo to his parents and announced his intention to marry her, they were overjoyed.

He and Moyo met in the first week of June, had brief premarital counseling in her church—*God's Word Assembly*—and got married in the church in November. She was thirty-one while he was thirty-two. Since he wasn't actively involved in his church, he didn't inform them about the wedding. As a result, only one person he regularly spoke with in the church attended.

Lolu had assumed that marriage meant he and Moyo would share more; that they'd have a joint account and enjoy regular sexual intimacy.

He had also thought that she would join him in his church. Even though he wasn't born again at the time they got married and didn't see church attendance as a big deal, he believed that he and his wife should attend the same church.

But no, things had not turned out that way. Moyo apparently had her own expectations and ideas about marriage.

When he brought up the topic of church, she argued that attending the same one wasn't necessary to please God or build a strong marriage. She explained that her church needed her, as she was actively serving in a department, and she wasn't willing to give that up.

Besides, she said she wasn't certain she liked his church or could fit in easily. She invited him to join her church instead, but because he'd heard some negative things about the current pastor of the church—Pastor Andrew—he declined. Also, even though he wasn't born again, somehow, he didn't think he should leave his church.

And so, every Sunday morning since they got married, they went their separate ways—he got in his car and went to his church while she went to hers in her car. And when their son was born, she took him along to her church as well.

When it came to finances, her stance remained unchanged—her money was hers alone, while his was meant for both of them. If she ever had to spend her own money on family expenses, she meticulously recorded it and sent him the bill for reimbursement. If he delayed repayment or was unable to cover it, she complained and got angry.

As for intimacy, she often had excuses, expecting him to understand. But he didn't—his patience wore thin, and his frustration turned into anger.

During the first two months of their marriage, he tolerated her excuses about sex. But when she conceived in February and insisted on being left alone, he reached his breaking point. He decided he'd had enough. A few weeks after, he began an affair with a woman who worked in an accounting firm near his office.

In June, about three months after the affair started, life had taken a hard turn. The company he worked for faced financial struggles and laid off several employees, including him.

It was a big blow, but he quickly picked himself up and three months after, in September, he started another job. The salary was a little more than what he earned where he previously worked, and this made him very happy; he would be able to maintain his family and the side relationship easily.

When Moyo gave birth to Jerry in October, he was elated and had an elaborate naming ceremony. Even his girlfriend attended, bringing along one of her friends, and they both took food and some pieces of meat home. He knew Moyo's temperament well enough to be certain that if she had discovered he was cheating and that the girlfriend and her friend were present at the ceremony, she would have caused a big scene.

Everything seemed to be going on well for Lolu … until about a year after, when the company he was working for could no longer pay staff salary.

When Jerry turned one in October, Lolu wanted to have a small celebration in the compound of the house they lived in, but Moyo wouldn't hear of it. She insisted on having a birthday party at an entertainment restaurant for children. Lolu didn't think it was necessary but eventually agreed when she said she wasn't going to take the money from him.

In December, when his job owed him four months' salary with no end in sight, he had no choice but to resign at the end of the month. Something wasn't right, he thought, greatly troubled.

It was at this point that he reached out to the pastor at his church. Desperation and frustration, coupled with the double life he was living, were wearing him down, and he needed help. Also, his savings account was almost empty.

He went to church on the second Sunday of January, and when the service ended, he headed for the pastor's office for the first time.

The pastor received him warmly and listened to his troubles with a patience that disarmed him. As the pastor counseled and prayed for him, his words touched something deep within Lolu's heart. The pastor spoke of true surrender—of Lolu giving not just his problems to Jesus, but also his life.

Lolu felt his heart crack open, and when the pastor asked if he would like to give his life to Jesus, he said yes. As Lolu prayed and made Jesus his personal Lord and Savior, he could feel the weight of his burdens begin to lift. Somehow, he knew that Jesus would help him, and everything would some day be okay.

While the pastor was asking him some questions and counseling him, Lolu admitted that he had been in the church for about three years but only came once or twice in a month.

Another question from the pastor made him confess that he had been cheating on his wife for over a year. He didn't hold anything back, and when the pastor told him he would need to end the ungodly relationship, he agreed without hesitation. He knew all along that the side relationship was wrong.

The pastor also wanted to know about his marriage and why his wife worshipped in another church but knowing that Moyo would not want him to discuss their marriage, Lolu simply said everything was under control, and that he would discuss the church matter with his wife.

Another reason he didn't want to say anything about his marriage was because during the short premarital counseling they had in Moyo's church, they were told not to involve anyone in their matter. Besides, their marriage was still young, and he had just become a Christian. He believed that with time, things would improve.

At home later that day, he told Moyo about his visit to the pastor, and that he had given his life to Jesus.

As he spoke, he felt a strong prompt in his heart to confess his infidelity and ask for her forgiveness, even though he knew God had already forgiven him. He was aware it would upset her, but he sensed it was the right thing to do, so he chose to go ahead with it.

As he had expected, Moyo was furious and shocked. He apologized deeply and promised to remain faithful to her going forward. She demanded to know how he planned to end the affair, and he assured her that he would immediately send a message to the woman, ending the relationship. He would also pray, stay away from her, and sever every tie.

After the long conversation, Lolu prayed for their family.

From that day, his spiritual journey began in earnest. In church, he was baptized in both water and the Holy Spirit. He attended the New Believers Class, immersing himself in learning and growth. He prayed and read the Bible regularly, and each day, as he felt stronger in his faith, a peace he hadn't known before began to settle within him.

Now convinced that he and Moyo were supposed to worship in the same church, he brought it up again. But to his surprise, she refused again. For the sake of peace however, he dropped the matter and began to pray with his family every evening.

In the meantime, he decided to take up a teaching job, and he started in June. It wasn't his dream job however, and he didn't feel fulfilled. He had never thought he would become a teacher, but the small salary allowed him to be able to meet some personal and family needs while he trusted God to open a better door.

Then, about three and a half months ago, in January, after some days of prayer, he decided to stop looking for a well-paying job, take a step of faith, and pursue photography—a passion he'd had since his university days. It was a risk, especially starting from scratch, but he felt God's peace about it. He went for training to hone his skills, purchased some necessary equipment, and began to work.

It was still early days though, and most of his clients were family and friends, who seemed to be more interested in helping him get practice than paying him. The few who did pay offered just enough to cover his basic expenses, but he didn't allow himself to get discouraged. He believed God would use this business to lift him in time. God would help him build something worthwhile through his vision, and he still held on to that faith.

But Moyo didn't see it that way. She had made it clear that she wanted him to get that well-paying and steady, nine-to-five job. She thought he was being reckless, letting go of a real job in pursuit of what she called a 'hobby'. To her, his decision was foolish, and a sign of irresponsibility. She couldn't understand why he would choose to struggle with something so uncertain, and each time she brought it up, it chipped away a bit more at the faith and hope he was trying so hard to hold on to.

This issue now seemed to be pulling at the seam of their already fragile relationship as things seemed to be getting worse. They were more like a couple sharing a home and life but moving along parallel paths that rarely touched.

Moyo had always been strong-willed, but lately, her words had become sharper, and her attitude colder. Respect was hard to find in her interactions with him, and her lack of care cut deep.

He had once suggested they go to his pastor and his wife for counseling, hoping that someone outside their home might help, but she had refused outrightly, dismissing the idea as unnecessary. When she said that, he had asked if she would want them to see the pastor in charge of her church even though he didn't believe in the man. Lolu was willing to do so if that would help them, but she had also said no to the idea, her reason being that she wouldn't want her church members to know what was going on in her marriage.

Since Lolu surrendered his life to Christ, he had been trying to make his marriage work and praying fervently for his family. Every day, he lifted up not only his son, but also his wife in prayer, hoping that one day his marriage would experience the peace and joy he longed for, and which God promised him in His word.

He had also committed to sharing God's word and praying with his family each night, believing that these moments could anchor them together, but there were nights he hesitated, feeling Moyo's resistance like a wall between them. Sometimes he didn't feel like praying with her. Even though she went to church regularly on Sundays and Thursdays, he couldn't help but wonder what she was learning there. He knew that the fruit of salvation is a changed life as his life had changed when he gave it to Jesus, but Moyo's behavior seemed unchanged. Maybe worse, and it troubled him deeply. Was she truly saved?!

Lolu took a deep breath. Why was his wife acting this way? Did she know how her attitude and words bruised him? Was she even aware of how much he was struggling to hold things together?

He wondered if he should report her to someone. He would love to but the fact that they had agreed not to involve anyone in their matter held him back.

Yet tonight, as he thought about Moyo, he felt this resolve weakening. Maybe it was time to let someone know what was going on, to find help before he or their marriage broke under the strain. Before things would fall apart.

How long could he keep enduring her behavior? He wasn't enjoying his marriage, and it hurt to admit it. At times, he felt she was deliberately trying to push him to his limits. Other times, he felt he was battling alone, and he wondered if his efforts even mattered.

Sitting there on the bed, he felt discouraged. There was a temptation to stop trying, to let go of the hope he was fighting to keep alive but reminding himself that he was a Christian and he must keep his eyes on Jesus and His word, he pushed the discouragement down, and away.

He began to pray quietly, asking God to touch his wife's heart, strengthen him, and strengthen his marriage.

Lolu's thoughts drifted to his son whom he loved very much. He had determined to raise his son to know the Lord, and to give him a good example to follow. He couldn't afford to be discouraged now, he counseled himself. No matter what was going on between him and Moyo, he had to protect his son and raise him for God. He must be a good example to him, he told himself, and that resolve steadied him.

He counseled himself to return to the living room and pray with his family. He must be strong and hold on to God's word and will.

Because his heart was heavy, he decided that he wouldn't share a Scripture as he usually did. He would simply pray.

With that decided, he stood up, took a deep breath, and returned to the living room.

Moyo and Jerry were still there.

"Can we pray now?" He announced in a calm but firm voice.

Moyo looked up from her phone and then set it aside.

He sat down, looked at their son, and said, "We want to pray."

Jerry went to bed early, but they allowed him to spend a little more time watching TV or playing with his toys on Fridays.

Reaching for the TV remote, Lolu pressed, and the screen blinked off, leaving silence in the room.

"Close your eyes." He told his son.

Jerry did, covering his face with his two hands.

Lolu bowed his head, closed his eyes, and began to pray. His words to God were simple and direct. He thanked the Lord for his family, and asked for the Lord's protection, provision, peace, and strength, over his home, in the name of Jesus.

When he finished, Moyo and Jerry said Amen.

Without another word, he got up, walked over to the main door, and gave it a quick check to be sure it was locked. Then, he made his way to the bedroom, closing the door gently behind him. He was ready to rest and face another day.

In bed however, he couldn't sleep as he kept thinking. He and Moyo needed to be on the same page and speak the same language if this marriage would work. For how long could he keep trying alone? He wondered, staring at the ceiling. What did he need to do?

****

Moyo stood, and led Jerry to the bathroom, her movements brisk and efficient as she guided him through his nightly routine.

In his room which had a child monitor with camera, she helped him into his pyjamas, tucked him into bed, and kissed his forehead before turning on his bedside lamp.

At the door, she switched off the overhead light, murmured a goodnight, and stepped out, leaving the door ajar. She and Lolu always kept Jerry's door open at night, allowing them to check on him easily or wake him to pee. Likewise, their own bedroom door remained slightly open, ensuring Jerry could find his way to them if he woke up before they did or needed comfort.

In their own bedroom, Moyo changed into her nightwear, and as she got in bed, she cast a glance at Lolu beside her. His eyes were closed and his body was turned slightly away but she was certain he wasn't asleep yet. Knowing he was still upset, she didn't bother to talk to him, and the silence between them remained heavy and unyielding.

****

With his face away from her, Lolu's thoughts drifted into familiar territory—wondering why things were going wrong between them.

What should I do, Lord? he prayed silently, trying to make sense of it all. They argued a lot and her attitude sometimes left him exhausted, yet he didn't regret marrying her. He loved her, and he believed in their marriage, but the frustration was real, lingering like a shadow in their home.

He remembered noticing before they got married that she kept a part of herself guarded. She had once shared with him that a past relationship had broken her heart, and that her father had been careless with money, leaving her with deep-seated fears. Lolu had thought he understood. He figured her past might explain some of her guardedness, and he had hoped she would see over time that he wasn't like those men who had hurt her. So he had chosen patience, trusting that in time, she would let down her walls. But now, it was clear that not much had changed.

When they'd first gotten married, he knew how much she earned even though she had refused to open a joint account, dismissing the idea as unnecessary. Her resistance had surprised him, but he had let it go, hoping they would grow into a place of shared trust. As time went on though, she began to give him various excuses whenever he tried to find out about her salary, and he had eventually stopped asking. He decided he would fulfill his responsibility regardless. He was the man; he would do his part to take care of his family, he told himself regularly.

And he had. Despite the difficulties with work and his transition to photography, he did all he could for her and their son. But her reaction—or lack of one—made him feel as though his efforts went unseen. The more he tried, the more he sensed her resistance, and the burden was becoming too much for him to bear.

I will need to talk to her again, he thought. They couldn't go on this way. If we're going to make this work, we need to be open with each other. Releasing a deep breath, he let the thoughts fade and with time drifted off to sleep, hoping the morning might bring clarity.

****

Moyo turned the light off, turned her back to Lolu, and adjusted herself to be comfortable. She closed her eyes, simmering quietly with her own frustrations. If he was upset with her, she was also upset with him. For how much longer would they keep this up, simply managing to get by?

She couldn't understand why he was still holding on to the teaching job and the photography business. Why would he think they were enough? Why would he treat them like his main job? He could do both on the side if he had wanted, but they couldn't support their household or the kind of life she wanted. She was certain his choice to go into photography had a lot to do with the fact that she had a stable, well-paying job, but that shouldn't be a reason to lean on her. How could he expect her to understand and support his idea? She wouldn't.

And there was the issue about her car. They used her car whenever they went anywhere together since her car was better than his. His car had developed some faults and was no longer reliable. Yet, each time they drove off in her vehicle, with him behind the wheel, she felt a mixture of resentment and regret. People would think he was the owner of the car, and that he was taking good care of her, not knowing that it wasn't so.

She had promised herself that she would marry a man with a good job. *How did I get here*? She asked herself for the umpteenth time.

She remembered her time as a single woman, when she could spend her money the way she liked, a time when things had seemed simpler.

As she lay in the dark and thought about the past, her mind wandered to the men in her life before Lolu came along.

There was James. He wasn't a very serious Christian, but they shared a deep connection and enjoyed being together. There was nothing she couldn't discuss with him, and they subsequently agreed to get married.

The General Overseer of *God's Word Assembly* had not relocated to Canada with his family, at the time. Moyo informed James that, as a church worker, she needed to tell the General Overseer about their relationship, and James agreed.

Before she had the chance, however, the General Overseer called her and mentioned having a dream about her. In the dream, Moyo was preparing to marry a man, but just weeks before the wedding, both she and the man were attacked by another man and left lifeless on the ground. The General Overseer believed the dream was a warning from God. He then asked Moyo if she was in a relationship, and when she confirmed, he advised her to pray, though he expressed doubts about her going forward with the relationship. He wanted to know more about James, and upon realizing that he was not genuinely born again, he advised Moyo to end the relationship.

Moyo, convinced the General Overseer was a true man of God, trusted that he was not trying to mislead her. She shared the General Overseer's words with James and her mother, then ultimately ended the relationship. Though she and James kept in touch for a while, their communication gradually faded away. Shortly after, when she changed her phone, she lost some contacts including his.

It was about this time that the General Overseer relocated with his family, and Pastor Andrew became the pastor in charge of the church.

After James, some men showed interest in Moyo but they were either married or non-Christians, and she knew better than to get involved with them.

Some months after, she met Kunmi who worked in an oil company and had a car that was better than hers. He had a five-year-old daughter and a baby mama drama, but Moyo believed she could cope. She truly loved him and thought they would get married, but his sudden termination of the relationship had left her heartbroken.

By the time Lolu came into her life a few months after that, she had become desperate to get married. When Lolu began to pursue her, she was happy and hopeful, and ready to compromise more of God's standards. He was the kind of man she had wanted—decent, level-headed, had a good job, and had no baby or baby mama drama. She knew he was not born again, but because she was eager to get married, she had entered into a relationship with him.

Now, Lolu was still decent and level-headed. He had also become a true Christian, but the good job was no longer there. That mattered a lot to her, and it was now a source of concern which she couldn't shake off.

Moyo sighed. She loved to dress well. In her office, she was known for her love of fashion, but in recent months, she'd had to consider Lolu and their situation, and tone things down.

Her background was contradictory though. She had been raised in a home where money was tight. Every necessity was a struggle, and she had promised herself that she wouldn't go through that again or let her children go through it.

Moyo's father had passed away about twelve years ago, but she knew that her parents' marriage had been far from happy before his death. Her father had once held a stable job, and life seemed fine until he developed a gambling habit and began coming home drunk. Eventually, he lost his job.

About six months later, he found new employment, but the salary was much lower. This didn't affect the family much, as he had stopped financially contributing after his habits started, leaving his wife to manage the household. Moyo's mother, who worked full-time and had started a business, took on the responsibility of running the home, paying the bills, and providing for the family. Though not a Christian at the time, she did everything she could to hold the family together.

Moyo's father often borrowed money from her mother, but despite never repaying it, she continued to lend him money, hoping he would eventually come to his senses and return to the man she once loved. Unfortunately, things only grew worse, and the financial strain on Moyo's mother became overwhelming. She began borrowing from friends and family to cover her children's school fees, promising to repay them when she received her salary at the end of the month. At times, she even took out loans to repay others, just to avoid the shame of not meeting her obligations.

For a long time, the woman hid the challenges in her marriage from her children, wanting to shield them from sadness and resentment toward their father. Though she was deeply unhappy, she put on a brave face, determined to protect them.

Moyo was in High School when she discovered she liked to fight for people. And with a sharp mind, natural curiosity, and ideas of her own, she decided she'd like to become a lawyer.

In the university, she faced significant challenges. Paying her tuition each semester was a constant struggle, and there were moments when she nearly had to drop out. To make ends meet, she started working part-time to cover her expenses.

It was in her final year when her father passed away. He was fifty two years old, and her mother, Abike, was forty eight. Moyo was almost twenty two. As the family made preparations for his burial, she promised herself that she would never let any man bring into her life the same troubles that her father had brought into her mother's. She vowed to work hard, earn her own money, and maintain control over her finances. Her money would be hers and hers alone.

Shortly after her father's burial, Moyo became a Christian and joined a campus fellowship. A few months later, she graduated from the university, passed her bar exam, and was fortunate to secure a position at the law firm, Gabriel Phillips & Co., where she still worked.

When she got the job, she made another important promise to herself: to take care of her mother. It was her way of rewarding her mother for all she had endured.

As Moyo remembered her father's recklessness, she told herself that she must not go back to that life. But with Lolu's choices, she feared it might be inevitable. And that upset her more.

She continued thinking. If only he would channel his energy and prayers to getting a good job, and be able to buy her expensive gifts, she would feel better and love him more. They wouldn't have to argue about money. She wouldn't feel that he was depending on her money, and she wouldn't feel this constant pressure. Even though she knew he was trying his best to provide for his family, his insistence on building a photography business was driving a wedge between them. Why couldn't he see how much easier things would be if he just found a well-paying stable job?

Opening her eyes, she stared at the ceiling even though the room was dark, and she couldn't see a thing. The room was silent, save for the soft hum of the air conditioner, and the ticking of the wall clock.

She could also hear Lolu's steady breathing, indicating he was now sleeping. Sleep eluded her, though.

As her thoughts spiraled, she could feel the pressure of the question growing inside her. "Did I marry the wrong man?" It was a thought that had been lingering in her mind; one she had pushed aside many times, hoping things would improve. But now, it hovered, demanding an answer.

She could see the good in him, and she knew he loved her and their son. But was love enough? Could it hold up under the strain of financial uncertainty and the frustration of clashing dreams?

Sighing, she adjusted herself and pulled the blanket up to her chin. She closed her eyes, and hoped that sleep would come soon and take her away from the questions that she had no answers to.

CHAPTER 3

ON SATURDAY MORNING, the light was just filtering through the curtains when Lolu woke up. He had an event to cover and after a brief prayer, he slipped out of bed.

As he moved around the room, gathering necessary things, Moyo stirred and blinked awake.

"Good morning." She greeted him.

He responded with the same brevity.

"Would you like to eat bread or noodles?" She asked, her voice flat with sleep.

"No, I'm fine. Thanks." He said, his tone neutral.

She spoke again. "I'll be using my car today."

"Okay." He replied. He hadn't planned on using it today anyway.

By 7:30am, he was ready. Slinging his camera bag over his shoulder, he paused by the bedroom door and glanced at her. "Alright, I'm off. Goodbye."

She had started using her phone, and barely looking up, she responded, "Bye. Have a nice day."

With a small nod, he left the apartment.

Once he settled into the driver's seat of his car, a familiar heaviness settled over him. His mind circled back to Moyo and the distance between them. He wasn't enjoying his marriage, and the realization stung.

Taking a deep breath, he thought of something to lift his spirit, and reached for a CD. Soon, gospel music poured out, filling the car. He started the car, and as he drove away, he began to sing along, letting the melody calm his mind.

Yahweh Sabaoth
Yahweh Sabaoth
The Lord of hosts
The King of glory
Yahweh Sabaoth
Yahweh Sabaoth

On the way to the event—a child's naming ceremony—he decided to stop at a small restaurant to eat, to avoid having to eat at the event since he wasn't sure about the food that might be served there. Besides, he preferred a quiet meal alone now, to clear his head before he would get to the event and start to work.

He didn't stay long at the restaurant, and by 9am, he arrived at the event's venue, an hour before the ceremony would commence, just as he liked it. Setting up his equipment, he soon lost himself in the work. The hours slipped by, and by 1.30pm, the event was wrapping up.

Just as he finished packing his things and prepared to leave the venue, his phone alerted him to a chat. He took the phone out of his shirt pocket, checked, and saw a message from Moyo.

I'll be going to Adesua's house this afternoon.

He sighed, and without responding, he slipped the phone back into his pocket.

As he walked toward his car, his mind wrestled with a decision: to head home or visit his parents? He knew he should go home, but the thought of the strain between him and Moyo made him hesitate.

By the time he reached his car, he had made up his mind to visit his parents instead. He needed a break—a few hours to relax and let go of the tension.

Pulling out his phone, he dialed his mother's number. "Hello, Mama?" He said when his mother answered.

"Lolu!" She exclaimed; a warm smile evident in her voice. "How are you?"

"I'm fine, Mama. Are you and Dad at home?"

"Yes, we're here. Why?" She sounded surprised, and that was because he'd just been there on Thursday. He was there last week as well.

"I'm planning to stop by." He said, smiling faintly.

"Oh, wonderful! I'm sure your father will be happy to see you again. Are you coming with your wife and son?"

"No."

"No? Why not?" She asked, a note of curiosity in her voice.

"Because they are not with me. I'm coming from an event I went to cover."

"Oh, I see. But is everything okay?"

"Yes, everything's fine. Just want to come over." He replied, keeping his tone casual. "Is there food?"

"Yes, I'm actually in the kitchen, cooking. It should be ready by the time you get here."

"Alright then. I'll be there soon." He said and hung up shortly after.

Settling into the driver's seat, he started the engine. As he drove toward his parents' house, he felt some form of uneasiness in his heart. He knew he should be going home. And he knew he'd been visiting his parents and friends more often lately. As he considered this, he had to admit it was because he wasn't very happy with Moyo, and he just needed to go somewhere that felt … safe; where he could relax and feel loved. Anything to get away from Moyo for a while.

As he drove on, memories of his wedding day drifted into his thoughts. He and Moyo had both been very happy, surrounded by friends and families, and he'd felt so sure they would face life's challenges and achievements together as one. But now, it seemed like Moyo's concerns about money were eating away at their oneness, casting shadows over moments that once brought them joy.

His mind wandered to his previous relationship, remembering the struggles that eventually led him to end it. It hadn't been easy, but he'd made peace with the decision.

Then he met Moyo, and he'd thought things would be different. For a while, they were.

He pushed the thoughts about his marriage aside, letting himself relax as he headed for the comfort of his parents' home.

Before he knew it, he had pulled up to his parents' house, parking on the street out front. He took a deep breath and stepped out of the car, grateful for a break from his thoughts and concerns.

His father opened the door of the small bungalow for him, and inside, he saw his mother in the kitchen, putting finishing touches on lunch.

She looked up with a smile as he entered the kitchen. "Lolu, you're here!" She greeted him warmly.

Lolu greeted her and then helped her to carry a bowl to the lunch table.

Within minutes, she announced, "Food is ready."

"Thanks, Mama." He replied.

Soon, the three of them were seated around the table, eating pounded yam with vegetable soup. His parents didn't ask too many questions, allowing him to just enjoy his food in peace.

His two younger sisters were married and lived in other states of the country.

After lunch, Lolu settled into the living room's three-seater sofa with a sigh, feeling a little lighter.

His mother glanced at him, sensing something. "You look tired, Lolu." She said gently.

He managed a small smile. "I am, Mama It's been a long day."

"Well, take your time to rest here. You know you're always welcome." His father chimed in, giving him a reassuring nod.

"Thank you, Dad." Lolu smiled, feeling grateful for their support.

At around three, he pulled out his camera and began sorting through the pictures he'd taken at the event, carefully selecting the best shots. He soon lost himself in the work, the hours passing peacefully in the familiar comfort of his parents' home.

****

After sending the message to her husband, Moyo started getting ready to go out, and finally left with her son around 3pm.

Her friend, thirty-two-year-old Adesua, was her maid of honor when she was getting married. Adesua was now married with a set of twin girls who were seventeen months old.

Adesua joined *God's Word Assembly* when the General Overseer was still around. Soon, she became close friends with Moyo and Nancy even though they were two years, and a year older than her respectively. But when Adesua had a conflict with the pastor in charge of the church after the relocation of the General Overseer, she left and returned to the church where her family members worshipped. And when she got married, she joined her husband's church.

Adesua and her husband, Tade, lived in a two-bedroom apartment but shortly before the birth of their twin girls, they moved into the three-bedroom apartment which they presently lived in, which was in a nice and quiet neighborhood.

Tade was a lawyer and worked in Adesua's father's law firm. Adesua's parents were rich, but Adesua did not depend on them. She had her own money as she was a TV presenter with her own show. Tade also earned a good salary at the law firm, and Adesua's father was grooming him to take over the law firm eventually.

When Moyo and her son arrived that afternoon, Adesua greeted them warmly, and ushered them into the living room of her elegantly decorated apartment.

When Moyo did not see Adesua's twins or husband in sight, she wanted to know where they were. Adesua said that her mother had come to spend a few days with her and was in the twins' room with the twins who were sleeping. Adesua's husband was not around, and the nanny that Adesua had employed from her parents' church had gone out to purchase some groceries. The nanny had been employed when Adesua knew it would be challenging for her to combine her work as a TV presenter with taking care of young twins. Her mother came around regularly to help, which she appreciated. If her mother-in-law were to be alive, she would have appreciated her support as well.

Moyo asked if she could go to the room to greet her mother, and Adesua said yes. With Jerry holding on to her hand, Moyo followed Adesua to the room, greeted Adesua's biracial mother, and returned to the living room.

Moyo walked to the three-seater sofa in the room, sat in a corner, and her son sat beside her.

Adesua soon set out a tray that contained a glass cup of cold water, cutleries, and a plate that contained fried rice, fried plantain, and a big fried fish.

"Help yourselves." She told Moyo and her son with a smile, and then joined them on the sofa, sitting in the second corner.

Moyo thanked her, blessed the food and water, and then carried the cup to take a sip.

Adesua asked Moyo, "How's your husband?"

Moyo shrugged. "Well, I guess he's fine." Taking a spoon, she took some rice and put the food in her son's mouth.

Adesua raised an eyebrow. "Why did you say it like that?" She asked Moyo with a curious smile.

"He got me upset last night." Moyo revealed and hissed as she began to eat.

"Really?" Adesua turned fully toward her and asked, "Why? What happened?"

Moyo sighed and then recounted the events from the night before—their quiet tension, and the way his decision about work was affecting her mood.

"I was just upset." She finished, and ate a piece of her fish.

Adesua nodded thoughtfully. "I understand. But Moyo, with the way things are right now, you need to support him. Encourage him and love him." She said gently. "If photography is what he wants to do, then maybe you just have to trust him on it and give it some time. He started just about three months ago."

Moyo frowned slightly, looking doubtful. "I really don't see how it will work."

"It will work." Adesua replied, her voice steady with conviction. "With your prayers, support, and encouragement. Some things need time to grow, you know."

"I know, but you don't know what I'm going through, Adesua. What my husband is making me go through." Moyo said and made a sound somewhere between a scoff and a groan, her expression a mixture of exasperation and disbelief.

Adesua chuckled, unable to hold back her amusement.

Moyo shot her a disapproving look, though a faint smile cracked through. "It's not funny." She said, trying to sound stern.

"I know, and I know what you're going through." Adesua replied as her laughter subsided.

Moyo shook her head. "I don't think you do."

Adesua met her gaze, with sincerity in her eyes. "I do."

Moyo sighed, unconvinced. "I doubt it. Yes, you know the story about my family, Adesua, but experiencing it … living it … it's different. There's no way you can fully understand. You were born and raised in the US; your parents are rich. You've never been in my shoes."

Adesua nodded slowly.

Moyo went on. "The problem is that Lolu is just like my father. My father took life easy; he was so laid back."

Adesua shook her head firmly. "No, I don't think he's like your dad at all. First of all, he's a Christian. Your dad wasn't. And from what you told me, your dad wasn't even working. But Lolu … he's working. He left the seemingly good job because they owed him four months' salary. From working in an office, he began to teach in a classroom. And now he's focusing on his own business, and he's good at it."

"He's good at it?" Moyo raised an eyebrow, crossing her arms. "Is that what will put food on our table and pay the rent?"

"It's a good business, Moyo. He just needs people to know him, and more money will come. You could introduce him to some of your friends."

Moyo rolled her eyes. "Introduce him to some of my friends and tell them that my husband is a photographer?!" She shook her head to decline. "Your parents are wealthy, Adesua, and your husband's a lawyer. You went on vacation last summer. My family couldn't leave Lagos. Lolu couldn't even afford to take us to Ibadan."

Adesua chuckled. "It is well." She said softly, trying to ease the tension,

Moyo continued. "Growing up, my family struggled. My mother did everything she could. She sold her things and borrowed money from family and friends just to pay our school fees. And all the while, my father was out there living his best life, without any care. My mother stayed and endured, but I'm not her, Adesua. I'm not going to live like that!" Moyo said firmly, with frustration written all over her face.

"I understand your point. You can let him know how you feel; let him know your concerns. Talk to him, but don't push him. And don't try to change him, that's my point. Money is not everything." Adesua counseled.

"I know, but it matters."

Adesua nodded. "Yes. Don't worry, Moyo. Put your trust in God. Pray more and support your husband. Everything will be fine, with time. He loves you."

Moyo leaned back. "I'm beginning to doubt that he loves me. If he loves me, he will do what will make me happy."

Adesua shook her head. "No, no, don't say that, Moyo."

Moyo went on. "He can't afford to buy me a good handbag, and when I buy it with my money, he gets upset! You should see the way he reacts when I buy something for myself. I'm just like ... when did it become a crime to spend my own money on myself?!"

Adesua chuckled. "I'm sure he means well. But let me ask you ... do you love your husband?"

"Do I love him?" Moyo thought for a moment. "Yes, I do."

"But ... are you *in love* with him?"

Moyo raised eyebrows. "Didn't I just answer that? Or is this different from the first question?"

Adesua nodded. "It's different, Moyo. They seem the same, but they're not."

"Hmm." Moyo looked away, thoughtful.

Adesua continued, her tone gentle. "You may need to pray about that. Being *in love with him* is what you need in order to make this work."

Moyo hesitated. "Can I be really honest with you?"

"Of course! That's why we're friends."

"Sometimes, I wonder if I did the right thing agreeing to marry him."

"Don't say that." Adesua said and shook her head. "That's one mistake some married people make, thinking maybe they married the wrong one. Instead, you need to appreciate what you have, hold on, and make your marriage work. With determination and prayer, it'll be fine."

Moyo sipped her drink and put the cup down.

"No one's perfect, you know?" Adesua said, with a slight smile crossing her face.

Moyo drew in a deep, steadying breath. "I know."

"My husband and I have had our share of challenges. One of the things that have been helping us is the choice we make, over and over, to remain committed to our marriage. And we are learning and growing together." Adesua told her, her gaze thoughtful.

Moyo was looking at Adesua, absorbing her words.

Adesua went on. "Marriage is work. Things will not automatically fall into place, we must put in the work, and we must believe that it's worth it. Marriage is not about perfection; it's about working together as one."

"Part of the problem is that we argue a lot. It's like we want different things, and we're going in different directions. I saw some of these things before we got married." Moyo confessed.

Adesua looked at her friend with compassion in her eyes. "If you had concerns, maybe ... you shouldn't have married him. There would be no offence if you had changed your mind because you realized that you were not compatible. As the saying goes ... *a broken relationship is better than a broken marriage.*"

"I know." Moyo nodded and sighed.

"But now," Adesua continued, "You're in it. You're married to him, and you owe it to yourself, to him, and to your son, to make it work."

"I'm trying … but … there have been times that I've wondered if we'd make it; if our marriage will last. There are times I wonder – is it worth it?"

Just then, the twins' room door opened, and Adesua and Moyo fell silent as Adesua's mother stepped out.

"Are they awake?" Adesua asked.

"No, they're still sleeping." Her mother replied.

She then inquired about Moyo's mother and family, exchanged pleasantries with her, and returned to the room.

When they heard the door close behind her, Adesua and Moyo continued their discussion.

Then Adesua said, "Moyo, can I tell you the truth? You've been focusing and dwelling on the wrong things. What you should be thinking of is what the Bible says about marriage; what you need to do to make your marriage work. Your marriage is still young."

"I'm trying."

"Keep trying. Keep thinking about the good times you've had with him; the things you love about him. Focus on his strength, not his weaknesses."

Moyo's voice softened. "You know, he had a good job then, Adesua. I never thought we'd be here. This financial challenge is … a shock to me. I didn't see it coming."

"Such is life," Adesua said with a shrug.

Moyo took a deep breath.

Adesua leaned forward, her voice gentle. "Well, I have another question for you, Moyo … and these questions are just to help you search your heart."

Moyo nodded slowly, bracing herself. "Okay."

Adesua looked at her, choosing her words carefully. "I know you loved your ex, Kunmi ... but do you still think of him?"

Moyo took a deep breath again, hesitating. "Sometimes," she finally admitted. Then, quickly, she added, "Not often ... and this conversation is strictly between us."

"Of course." Adesua assured her. "But here's the thing, Moyo: while your ex still has a place in your heart, you can't fully love your husband. Besides, you're thinking about the wrong man. If Kunmi truly loved you, and if it was a good relationship ... why did he leave you?"

Moyo thought about it, letting Adesua's words sink in. She knew there had been many problems in her relationship with Kunmi. He'd taken her for granted, expecting her to be there no matter what. But she'd stayed patient and hopeful, because she'd loved him deeply. She'd never have spoken to Kunmi the way she sometimes spoke to Lolu—that much she knew.

As her mind shifted to Lolu, she realized she hadn't given him the appreciation he deserved. He was interested in her life, always asking about her job and her day. When he had money, he was generous to her. He was caring, good-looking, and a true child of God. No smoking, no drinking.

If he wasn't at home, he was at work, at church, with friends, or visiting family. He was reliable.

The only issue was their finance. She didn't like having to shoulder certain responsibilities or being told how to spend her own money. She didn't like that the sense of security she thought would come with marriage was lacking.

Adesua spoke up, breaking into her thoughts. "You know, Moyo, sometimes we don't see the blessing in front of us because we're holding onto shadows of the past. Lolu may not have everything together yet, but he's trying. And he's there for you. That's worth appreciating."

Moyo nodded, feeling a quiet sense of conviction. "Thank you." Then deciding she had heard enough, she smiled and said, "Well, enough about me. What's been happening to you?"

Adesua chuckled, her eyes twinkling. "Well, what's happening is ... it seems that I'm pregnant again."

"What?!" Moyo exclaimed.

Adesua laughed and nodded. "Umm hmm."

"Oh wow!" Moyo's eyes widened in surprise. "I thought you said you didn't want more children after the twins!"

Adesua laughed. "Yes, that's what I said! Honestly, I have no idea how this happened. Even my husband was surprised when I told him on Tuesday. But, well, what can we do? We just have to accept it."

"Wow!" Moyo said and smiled warmly. "Congratulations, Adesua."

"Thank you." Adesua reached out, and they clasped hands, smiling at each other.

Moyo had intended to conceive when Jerry turned two. Now, he was two and a half, yet she had not conceived. She wasn't concerned, though; in fact, she saw the delay as a possible blessing in disguise, given Lolu's financial situation.

Before she got up to leave, Adesua prayed, thanking God for their families, and asking Him for His guidance and strength in the days ahead, in the name of Jesus.

On her way home around 5.30pm, Moyo took out her phone and called Lolu. "Are you back home yet?"

To her surprise, he answered, "No, not yet."

She stopped at a store to buy some groceries with the money that Lolu brought home yesterday, and at home, she went to the kitchen.

As she began to cook, Adesua's words replayed in her mind. Yes, Lolu wasn't like her father. Whenever he borrowed money from her, he always repaid it—unlike her father.

She could still recall their conversation the first time he had asked her for a loan.

"I promise to pay it back when I get my salary." He had said.

She had scoffed, unimpressed. She had heard that line before. Her father had never returned the money he took from her mother, and she doubted Lolu would be any different.

"No way. Loan you? How many husbands actually return the money they borrow from their wives?" She had challenged.

"I promise to pay you back. I give you my word. I'm a Christian." He had assured her.

In the end, she had lent him the money, and true to his word, he had repaid it.

She also remembered the words he had spoken when he proposed: "I am the man. I will do my part to take care of you."

She had to admit that he had been trying to do things for her.

Before they got married, all the times they went out for lunch or dinner, he paid. She hadn't offered to pay actually and was glad that he paid. He wasn't the kind of man that onc of her cousins told her about. Her cousin and the man had met for lunch. When the bill was brought, the man said he didn't have much money on him, and her cousin was forced to pay. When they were parting, the man asked the lady for transport fare. She still paid, trying to check her spirit if God was testing her patience and love. When they met again, and the man asked her for a loan, she knew that was the end. The man was a parasite, not the will of God. Lolu hadn't been like that though, she must admit.

CHAPTER 4

AFTER A FEW minutes, Lolu felt his eyelids growing heavy. As he shut down his laptop, he announced, "I'm feeling sleepy. I'll just relax for a bit."

"You can go and sleep in the room you used before." His mother offered. "The bedsheet is clean."

"I'm fine here. Are you expecting any visitor?" He wanted to know.

His mother shook her head. "No, we're not expecting anyone."

"Then I'll just lie down here." He replied, settling deeper into the three-seater sofa.

"You can turn the TV off." His father suggested to his mother.

His mother nodded. "We're not really watching it anyway."

"It's not necessary." Lolu said. "The noise won't bother me."

"There's nothing interesting on right now." His mother picked up the remote and turned the TV off.

Lolu stretched out on the sofa, resting his head on the armrest. He moved around a bit to make himself comfortable, and before long, he drifted off to sleep.

When he woke up later and opened his eyes, he saw his mother reading her Bible while his father was on the phone.

His mother looked up. "You're awake."

"Yes." Lolu said as he sat up. He glanced at the time and realized it was already 6pm. "I'll be leaving soon."

"I'm cooking some jollof rice." She informed him. "It'll be ready soon, and you can take some home."

He shook his head. "No, that's not necessary. I'll just eat a little here before I go."

His father's phone call ended, and he put the phone down on the table in front of him.

When Lolu's mother went to the kitchen to check the food, his father called him.

"Yes, Dad?"

"You're supposed to be home by now. Why are you still here? Is everything okay?"

Lolu was taken aback; he'd forgotten just how observant his parents could be. "Everything's fine." He replied.

He hesitated, and then added, "Well ... maybe just one or two misunderstandings."

His father looked at him thoughtfully. "I'd advise you talk to your pastor if these misunderstandings are becoming issues of concern. Or have you done that already?"

Lolu shook his head, brushing it off. "No, it's not that serious. I can handle it."

Realizing that was not an honest answer as things were becoming serious, he thought of what to say to correct it without revealing much. "I mean … everything will be fine."

His father didn't talk.

Lolu looked at him and saw that he was watching him carefully, as if weighing Lolu's response.

On his way home about thirty minutes later, Lolu thought about the conversation with his father. Should he forget about his agreement with Moyo not to involve a third party? Should he talk to someone? If yes, who? He didn't think he should talk to his pastor yet. And Moyo might not want him to involve his friends. But what about her own friends? Adesua perhaps, or Nancy?

He finally told himself that it might not be necessary yet. He should be able to handle his home, after all, he was the husband. He had already decided to talk to Moyo again, and he would.

****

On Sunday morning, Moyo left home early with Jerry to attend her church, *God's Word Assembly*. She liked the church because of its location in a highbrow area, and because it was filled with young professionals, business owners, and wealthy individuals - connections she found valuable. The General Overseer of the church was a devoted man of God, but after relocating to Canada with his family for personal reasons, leadership passed to Andrew. Under

Andrew's guidance, several structural changes were introduced. One notable adjustment he made was reducing mid-week services from twice a week to once, on Thursdays, citing the busy schedules of the congregation.

****

Lolu left shortly after as his church was just a short drive away. Being a worker, he got to church about an hour before the service would start and joined his departmental members for prayer.

At the right time, the main service started with prayer. This was followed by praise and worship and soon the sound of musical instruments and joyful voices filled the air. From where he stood, he could see people as they arrived and were greeted by smiling ushers. The service went well as always, and on his way home around 1.30pm, he was humming one of the songs that the choir sang.

Moyo and Jerry were not yet back, and after changing his clothes, he went to the kitchen to boil some rice for the three of them to eat.

When they arrived, they ate, and shortly after, Moyo went to a salon to get her hair braided.

At around 5.30pm, Lolu was in the living room telling his son the story of David and Goliath from a children's Bible with pictures, when his phone began to ring. It was his friend, Timothy, and he answered it.

"I'm in your neighborhood to see a colleague. Are you at home?" Timothy wanted to know.

"Yes, sure." Lolu answered.

"Okay. I'll see you soon."

After the call, Lolu glanced around the living room. It was tidy except for a toy lying on one of the ottomans. He stood, picked it up, and placed it in the toy storage bin.

Returning to his seat, his thoughts drifted to whether he should talk to his friend about his struggles with Moyo or not. The friend was also married and a sound Christian.

He picked up the children's Bible he was using and continued reading to Jerry. By the time Timothy arrived, Lolu had decided against talking about his marriage, but figured he could at least get his opinion about his business.

He greeted Timothy with a broad smile and served him soft drink. They chatted casually for some minutes, and then Lolu eased into the topic.

"So," he began, a bit hesitant, "I'm wondering about my photography business ... should I pack it up? What do you think?"

Timothy raised an eyebrow. "Why would you do that? I thought things were going okay."

"Well, they are, sort of. But you know, it's just slow, and Moyo's getting frustrated. She's wondering if it'll ever really take off." Lolu admitted, his tone contemplative. "She also thinks that it's not dignifying."

Timothy nodded, thoughtful. "Look, I get it, but a lot of businesses start slow. The question is … are you seeing any growth?"

"Yeah, there's growth … just not enough to be where I'd like to be yet." Lolu admitted, leaning back on the sofa.

Timothy gave him an encouraging smile. "Maybe instead of packing up, you just need a new strategy. Think about networking more and marketing a bit differently. It sounds like you've got something good, just not everyone knows about it yet."

Lolu considered this, feeling a glimmer of hope. "Hmm, maybe you're right."

"Your wife has a good job. With her support, prayer, and patience, you'll grow."

Lolu simply smiled, not wanting to tell his friend about his wife's opinion and behavior these days.

In bed later at night, he told Moyo that he'd want them to talk, and he began the conversation. It started well, but when they began to argue, he stopped talking and turned his back on her.

****

On Monday morning, as usual, Moyo fed her son and got him ready before leaving for work. Her husband would drop him off at preschool on his way to the High School where he taught.

She wore a beautiful black and white dress, and with her braided hair nicely piled on top of her head, she left the house. By 8.05am, she arrived at her office and quickly settled in.

She loved her job. Being a strong person, she was a tough lawyer. However, she was gentle, loving, and devoted to her son, Jerry. She knew she was supposed to be the same to her husband, but she regularly reminded herself that she must be tough with Lolu so he would not take advantage of her.

****

That Monday, Lolu arrived home with Jerry around six in the evening. As he worked on his laptop, his phone began to make a continuous sound with WhatsApp notifications. Picking it up, he saw that his High School group chat was in the middle of a discussion about marriage.

One of the members, a man who was still unmarried, had posted a comment dismissing marriage entirely.

Honestly, I don't think marriage is worth it. All you hear are stories of problems and regrets. Why even bother?

A few others chimed in with similar sentiments, echoing his disillusionment.

One said:

Marriages just seem to go downhill after a while. Too much drama.

Another commented:

People change when they get married. It's not worth the headache.

Only two people spoke up in support of marriage. One was a man who wasn't a Christian, and while his message was supportive, it wasn't exactly encouraging. He had tried to sound positive, but the words lacked conviction.

Marriage is okay if you find the right person ... but don't expect much. Just go with the flow.

The second comment, however, came from someone who spoke more positively:

Marriage can be fulfilling if both people are committed and ready to grow together. It's not perfect, but it has its blessings.

Lolu felt prompted to add his own perspective, and began to type:

*Marriage is a good thing. It doesn't matter what you see or hear about it; the word of God stands sure. Put your trust in God and you'll be fine. The Bible says in **Ecclesiastes 4:9-12,***

"Two are better than one, because they have a good reward for their toil. For if they fall, one will lift up his fellow. But woe to him who is alone when he falls and has not another to lift him up."

As he continued typing thoughtfully, doubt crept into his mind. He thought about the challenges in his own marriage. Wasn't it hypocritical for him to say marriage was good when his marriage was struggling?!

He considered stopping and deleting what he had typed, but then he told himself that he wasn't promoting his own experience, he was pointing the people to God's truth, and that was the right thing to do. A Christian should say what the Bible says.

He continued typing, choosing his words with care. He also added a verse that had been in his heart since morning:

Then the Lord God said, 'It is not good that the man should be alone; I will make him a helper fit for him. Genesis 2:18.

This is God's word that speaks God's mind or intent — marriage is good; it's a blessing. Despite what people may say or experience, we can trust God's word.

As he reread what he had typed, another scripture occurred to him, and he added it.

When he finished, he read through to be sure it was error-free. Satisfied, he pressed *Send* and hoped that his words would encourage the other members of the group.

Afterward, he leaned back, closed his eyes, and began to pray for his marriage, asking God for divine intervention, peace of mind, and strength for him to continue to hold on to the unwavering promises of God.

****

That Monday evening, it occurred to Moyo that Lolu might stumble on or insist on seeing her bank account statements one of these days, and the thought unsettled her.

Deciding to prepare, she went to a bank on Tuesday to open an account, one she wouldn't tell him about. She knew it wasn't right, but she told herself that she had to. She must be smart and plan her life as she wouldn't want to end up struggling like her mother.

While she waited in line to be attended to at the bank, she heard a familiar voice calling her name. She turned and, to her surprise, saw James, her ex. He looked as polished as ever, dressed in a black suit and crisp white shirt. It was clear he was doing well.

"James! Long time!" She greeted with a broad smile.

"You can say that again. It's really been a while." He replied, his smile wide and warm. "You look great. Heard you're married."

"Yes. And I heard you're still unmarried."

They both laughed.

"Moyosore," He usually called her by her full name when they were in a relationship. With his gaze still lingering on her, he exclaimed, "Wow! Marriage must be treating you well"

She nodded politely and said thank you, trying to keep her tone light even though she was wondering - when a married woman looks good, why do people assume that her husband is the one taking care of her?

He continued, "I'm sure your husband is taking good care of you. How many kids do you have now?"

Moyo hesitated. "We have one."

James nodded approvingly. "Nice, nice. Look, how about lunch sometime? It would be good to catch up."

She felt a moment's hesitation but decided to give a polite response. "Okay." She said, though she knew it might not be appropriate.

"Are you still using the same phone number?" He asked, his expression casual.

"Yes." She replied, nodding.

"Good." He said with a slight smile. "I'll give you a call."

"Alright." She answered, though her heart raced with a mix of emotions. "I'll expect your call."

As he walked away toward the bank manager's office and she looked at him, she felt a strange blend of nostalgia and uncertainty swirling in her mind. It was just last week that she thought of him, and now he suddenly showed up where she was. *How strange!*

About forty five minutes after, she had been attended to, and she left with some documents, to return to her office.

There, she sent a message to the WhatsApp group she had with Adesua and Nancy, to inform them that she saw James at a bank.

Adesua responded:

Did he see you? Did you talk?

Yes, he was the one who saw me and called me. He seems to be doing well.

Good for him.

On her way home in the evening, she called her mother. Her mother answered after a few rings, and they greeted.

"I just wanted to check on you." Moyo said.

"Thank you, my dear. How are Lolu and Jerry?"

"They're fine. Everyone is fine."

After exchanging more pleasantries, Moyo spoke again. "I'm thinking of buying a lace fabric for you for Mother's Day. What color would you like?"

"Ah, lace fabric? That's so thoughtful of you. God bless you."

Moyo said *Amen* and asked again, "What color would you like?"

"Well, any color is okay, but if they have fuchsia pink, I'd prefer that."

Moyo said okay, but her mother's next question made her heart sink a little.

"Will you buy the same color for your mother-in-law so we can wear it whenever we have to attend a ceremony together?"

Moyo sighed. "Mommy, I can't buy two."

"Why not? If money is tight, don't worry about getting it for me. But if you can afford it, I'd like you to buy one for her too. You have a wonderful mother-in-law, you know. That woman is nice, or … is there a problem?"

"No, there's no problem." Moyo answered.

"Some mothers-in-law are not very pleasant, I'm sure you know that. You should be thankful for the one you have."

"Well, if Lolu gives me the money for his mom's, I'll buy it."

"He doesn't have to. If he can't afford it, then you should. The woman is your mother-in-law."

Moyo sighed again. "Okay, Mom."

At home in her bedroom, she hid the bank documents in her closet, among her clothes.

Since it was Tuesday, Lolu took his son to church for Bible study. The service began at 6pm and ended at 8pm.

When they returned home, Moyo brought up the issue with her husband. "I'd like us to buy lace fabric for my mom and yours for Mother's Day."

"How much will it cost for both of them?" Lolu asked.

Moyo shared the price with him.

He frowned. "That's too much. Why don't you buy something less expensive?"

"This isn't expensive, Lolu. It's very reasonable. I wouldn't want us to buy a cheap fabric for either of them."

When he insisted it was expensive, she said, "Alright, don't worry about my mom. Just give me the money for your mom's."

"Well, I don't have that kind of money now. We have bills to pay, you know. I'd suggest we get something else for them. My mom will appreciate whatever we give her, even if it's Ankara."

When Moyo didn't respond, he knew she must be upset.

After about three minutes, he spoke again. "Okay, here's what we'll do—buy the lace fabric for both of them and note it down. I promise to repay you for both gifts as soon as possible. I'm expecting some money soon."

She remained silent, pondering his suggestion. True, he had been repaying the money he borrowed from her, but never on time. However, unless his financial situation improved significantly, a time would come when he might not be able to pay her back at all. And if he didn't, what could she do? Where would that leave her?

"I don't even have any money now." She lied.

"Forget about the lace then. We can give them something else."

She knew he would say that.

Silence hung between them for about a minute before he spoke again. "But what do you mean by you don't have any money? What have you been doing with your money?"

She avoided his gaze as she answered, "I've been paying off my loan. Remember?"

"I thought you said that loan was finished."

"No." She said.

That loan had been repaid, but she had taken another one to buy a piece of land, without telling him. She planned to tell him later, when the time felt right.

Later in bed, her mind wandered to her ex, Kunmi. During their brief relationship, she never hesitated to do things for him. He hadn't even needed to ask; she simply did them because she wanted to.

But that was the past, she counseled herself. She was married to the man lying beside her, not Kunmi.

She sighed. But just as she pushed Kunmi out of her mind, the face of James appeared. She could still remember the excitement she felt at seeing him, and the way he smiled as he looked at her. Why did he ask to have lunch with her? And what should she say if he called? She might have to lie.

That was when she remembered that she lied to Lolu earlier on. She lied a lot these days, she realized. Closing her eyes, she asked the Lord to forgive her for lying, and give her peace in her marriage.

After a few minutes, her thoughts drifted to the lace fabric. She recalled her mother's advice to buy it for Lolu's mother as well, and she frowned. *Why should I?*

She decided not to buy the lace for either of them.

On her way to work the next morning though, she reconsidered. Her mother was involved, after all. She opted instead to buy Ankara fabric for both women.

But then another thought struck her. How could she not give her mother the exact gift she desired to give her? Why should she settle for Ankara just because of Lolu's mother? Besides, she had already mentioned the lace to her mother, who had thanked her in advance. Resolving the matter, she chose to buy lace for her mother and Ankara for her mother-in-law.

The next day, Thursday, she managed to leave the office at 4.10pm. She drove straight to the store, and bought lace fabric for her mother and Ankara for Lolu's mother. She also picked up the phone handset she had promised her mother.

From there, she headed to *God's Word Assembly,* for midweek service.

Lolu called to let her know he was on his way to his church's prayer service.

She returned home before Lolu and Jerry. Wasting no time, she quickly wrapped her mother's gifts so Lolu wouldn't see them.

When he arrived, she showed him the Ankara fabric for his mother before wrapping it, and he thanked her for the thoughtful gesture.

The second Sunday of the month of May was Mother's Day, and they both went to their churches.

Back at home in the afternoon, they had lunch, and then set off to visit his mother first, with the neatly wrapped and labelled gifts on the backseat, beside Jerry's car seat.

When they arrived, Lolu's mother greeted them warmly at the door, her face lighting up at the sight of his son and his family.

"Ah, welcome! Come in, come in." She exclaimed, ushering them inside. She had freshly fried chinchin waiting for them, and the aroma wafted through the air.

Lolu's father was in the living room, and they greeted him.

After some pleasantries and laughter, Moyo retrieved the wrapped fabric from her handbag. "Mama, happy Mother's Day." She said, handing over the gift with a smile.

Lolu's mother thanked her and Lolu. With eager hands, she unwrapped the package and saw the Ankara fabric. "Ah, this is beautiful! Thank you. God will bless you both abundantly, in Jesus' name."

They ate some chinchin and when they were ready to leave, Lolu's mother put some chinchin in a takeaway bowl with lid, for them to take home.

From there, they made their way to Moyo's mother's house. The woman had cooked, and they sat down to eat.

They were still eating when Moyo's younger brother, Alfred, arrived with his family. It was clear that Alfred bore a striking resemblance to their father, while Moyo took after their mother.

Alfred and his family joined the table, blending into the lively atmosphere as conversation and laughter flowed. Moyo had two more younger siblings, and their mother mentioned that they had called earlier, promising to arrive later in the day.

When Moyo was ready to leave with her family, she went to her mother and handed over the wrapped package. She knew that her mother would not open the gift immediately, unlike Lolu's mother. Her mother would also not ask any question in Lolu's presence; she would save her inquiries for a more private moment. And that was what happened.

Her mother's eyes flickered briefly with curiosity but quickly softened as she accepted the gift with a smile. She thanked both of them and prayed for them without any question.

Shortly after, Moyo and her husband and son said their goodbyes, and left.

At about 7pm, Moyo was ironing the skirt she would wear to the office the next day when she received her mother's text. She wanted to know if Moyo bought the same color of lace for her mother-in-law, and she replied *No*.

She sent another text to Moyo to know the color of lace she bought for the woman, and Moyo confessed that she bought Ankara.

Her mother sent another text:

Why would you do that, after what I told you?

Moyo replied:

It's okay, Mom. I know what I'm doing.

Her mother did not respond.

CHAPTER 5

A WEEK AFTER, at about 5.30pm on Thursday, Moyo left a client's office, entered her car, and drove in the direction of her church for midweek service. When she reached a traffic light, she stopped, and glanced around briefly. The streets were bustling with activities—vendors hawking bottled water, food, and fruits, impatient drivers honking, and pedestrians weaving through the chaos.

Taking her phone from her black handbag, she pressed some buttons, and a gospel tune began to play inside her car. She returned the phone to her bag, started to drum her fingers on the steering wheel and hum softly to the music.

We are a chosen generation, called forth to show His excellence

All I require for life God has given me, And I know who I am

I know who God says I am, What He says I am

Where He says I'm at, I know who I am

I'm walking in power, I walk in miracles

I live a life of favor, For I know who I am ...

When the light turned green, she eased her car forward and merged onto the main road.

That was when she noticed a sleek deep blue metallic car beside her. As she returned her gaze to the front, she saw the car's window rolling down. She looked back and saw James, her ex. Her heart skipped a beat.

He waved at her.

She rolled down her side window as well and waved back.

"How are you?" He shouted.

"I'm fine. And you?"

"Great!" He said and waved again.

Before she could say any other thing, his car surged forward.

As it overtook hers, she recognized it to be Nissan Murano. She looked at the car as it sped off and soon the taillights disappeared into the distance.

A sigh escaped her lips. "Hmm. That's an expensive car." She muttered, her thoughts swirling. Her husband didn't drive anything close to that. She wondered where James worked now.

Just then, her phone, which was in her handbag began to ring, jolting her from her thoughts. She reached out and took it. Glancing at the screen, her breath hitched. The number wasn't saved, but it ended with 7070 and she recognized it immediately.

James! She whispered, her heart pounding. Why was he calling her now?

With nervous excitement, she pressed the answer button. "Hello?"

"Moyosore. How are you?"

She didn't need to ask who it was. "I'm good, James. How about you?"

"I've been well. Good to see you again."

"That's a nice car you drive." She told him.

"Thank you."

"Are you still at the advertising agency?"

"No, I have my own business now." He answered.

"Wow! Awesome!"

"Thanks. So … when can we have lunch or dinner? It'd be nice to catch up." He said, his voice smooth and persuasive.

Moyo chuckled nervously. She was tempted to suggest 'this weekend', but a quiet voice inside her whispered, *You're married. This isn't right!*

"I'm married." She said after a pause. "Can I come with my husband?"

James laughed lightly. "What's my business with your husband?"

She laughed too, though uneasily. "James!"

"I don't mean any disrespect, but that's just the truth." He said.

There was a pause for some seconds, then he spoke again, "Let's have dinner, for old time's sake."

Moyo hesitated, torn between curiosity and caution. "I'll think about it and let you know." She finally said, her tone non-committal.

"Alright. I'll expect your call. Enjoy your day." He told her.

She soon reached her destination, and after parking her car, she took her phone and saved James' number.

On her way home around 9.10pm, she called Adesua and Nancy to tell them that she saw James again.

James, again?! Her friends asked in unison.

Moyo laughed. "I'm also surprised. Just suddenly, he appeared from nowhere, and now I've seen him twice."

They wanted to know where she saw him today, and she told them.

In church on Sunday, there was a guest minister, and when the man began to preach, his words cut straight to Moyo's heart. His sermon on gratitude and cherishing one's blessings resonated deeply with her.

As the preacher continued preaching, talking about the dangers of comparison and taking loved ones, especially spouses, for granted, Moyo was overcome with conviction.

She thought of Lolu and his gentle patience, his quiet acts of love, and his unwavering support. She suddenly realized she'd been so focused on what he didn't have that she'd overlooked what he had, and what he had brought into her life. He had brought stability, kindness, a steadfast commitment, and a family she could call her own.

When the sermon ended and prayer began, tears stung her eyes as she whispered a prayer of repentance, asking God to help her refocus on her marriage and show love to her husband.

She decided to change immediately. Soon, the prayer session ended, and while announcements were being made, she began to think of how she could show love to her husband today.

On the way home, she stopped at a store to buy groceries, so she could cook something special for her family. Afterward, she drove to a restaurant and bought food that they would eat at home. Knowing that Lolu liked stockfish and snails, she bought them, and as she walked out of the restaurant with her son, and the bag of takeout food, she smiled a little, imagining the quiet wonderful evening ahead.

Inside the car, with the bag of takeout on the front passenger seat, and her son in his car seat at the back, she took her phone. She called Lolu and told him she had bought lunch and would be home shortly. She said she also bought groceries, and he asked if she would need help carrying them. When she said yes, he said she should call him when she was about three minutes away.

Soon, she gave him a call, and when she reached home, she found him waiting in the compound. She parked her car, and he walked over to assist her.

Inside the apartment, she quickly changed her clothes and returned to the living room. "Let me set it up."

She went to the kitchen to unpack the food, transferring it from plastic containers into plates. Lolu joined her and soon, she and Lolu were sitting shoulder to shoulder on the sofa, eating rice, chicken, snails, and stockfish while the TV was murmuring in the background. Jerry was seated on his chair, eating the food she served him.

As Lolu ate, he wondered what had changed.

When they were through, they cleaned up the tables, and back in the living room, she sat beside him.

Without a word, she reached out and took his hand in hers, squeezing it gently.

He looked at her, surprised. "What's this about?"

She shook her head, and then said, "Thank you."

"For what?" He asked, puzzled.

"For being you." She replied softly, resting her head on his shoulder.

He smiled. "It's good to hear that."

She began to use her fingers to trace slow deliberate patterns along his chest.

He looked at her, and she smiled. He returned the smile, understanding her unspoken message.

"Let's wait." He whispered and pointed at Jerry.

Jerry was playing with some toys. When he stopped and yawned, Moyo smiled and asked him, "Are you feeling sleepy?"

Jerry nodded, and she asked him to come over. She carried him, and within minutes, he was asleep. She made him comfortable on his foldable floor bed, and then she and Lolu quietly slipped into their bedroom.

In the evening, she went to the kitchen to cook, and soon, the aroma of fried fish filled the apartment. As she prepared his favorite dish, she hummed softly to herself.

Lolu went to her and as he held her by the waist, he asked if she would need his help.

"No, I don't think so."

He could see savory stew that contained snails and stockfish simmering on the stove. He gave her a peck and returned to the living room to work on his laptop.

As she continued cooking, she thought about the man she had married. He wasn't perfect, but he was solid—a man who loved the Lord, loved her, and would never strike her. He adored their son, carried his weight at home without complaint, and treated her family—mother and siblings—like his own.

"Lord, thank You for my husband." She prayed in almost a whisper. "Help me be the wife he needs, and give him strength to overcome whatever challenge he may face in Jesus' name."

As she continued praying, she resolved to keep praying for her husband, knowing that a love like theirs deserved to be nurtured, cherished, and protected.

She also decided to stop withholding her money. That week, she paid the electricity bill and Jerry's preschool's quarterly tuition.

****

Two Sundays later, around 5pm, Moyo was on the phone with Adesua and Nancy, and they laughed as they had a lively conversation. She was at home alone with her son as Lolu had gone out to cover an event.

Then Nancy announced that her family would be going on vacation to Canada on the first day of the following month, July. This would be the second time of going on vacation with her family since she got married a month after Moyo's wedding.

Adesua went on vacation regularly before she got married and had continued to do so after wedding.

"That's wonderful." Adesua chimed in. "My family will be going as well. We haven't booked our tickets, but it's going to be in July."

Moyo wanted to know when they would return as her birthday was on the twenty fourth of July, a Saturday. She would be turning thirty-five and would like them to come to her house. Nancy said she would be back by July 14, and Adesua said she had to be back by July 18 because of her TV show.

As Moyo listened and discussed with them, a trace of envy stirred within her, and she decided she would need to talk to her husband about their finances again.

Shortly after the call, her phone rang. The name on the screen made her pause—James.

She debated whether to answer, but curiosity won. "Hello?"

"Moyosore," James' deep voice greeted her. "I've been waiting for your call … about our lunch."

"Oh yes. I've not forgotten. It's just that … I've been busy."

"Well, how about it? Let's fix a time now."

She hesitated as her mind went to her husband. "Er - I can't commit to anything right now. I'll think about it and let you know."

"That was what you said the other time, but you didn't call. Are you trying to avoid me?"

She laughed. "Er, not really. It's just that I've been busy. Don't worry, I'll contact you soon."

They talked for about two minutes more, and when the call ended, she sighed. Reconnecting with him would only stir up trouble. What good would it do her?! And how could having dinner with her ex be right, especially bchind her husband's back? She wondered.

Lolu arrived at about 7pm. She gave him food and sat quietly, waiting for him to finish eating. When he did, he carried his plate to the kitchen and washed it. Back in the living room, he took his phone to respond to some messages.

Moyo spoke. "Nancy and her family will be going on vacation next month. Adesua will also be going with her family."

I'm too tired for this, Lolu thought as he continued using his phone.

Moyo was looking at him, and it was as if he did not hear her or her words had floated past him, but she knew he heard her.

She exhaled sharply and began again, "Nancy and her family will be going on vacation. Adesua will also be going with her family." Her tone was measured but pointed.

Knowing he should say something, he said, "Okay." But he barely looked up.

She pressed on, her eyes narrowing. "I'd like us to be able to go on vacation too. Everything is boring sometimes; I need some fun."

He took a deep breath but didn't say a word.

"Did you hear me at all?"

"Yes, I did." He replied without looking at her.

"So, what about us?" She folded her arms.

Lolu finally glanced up. "We will also." He said quietly, then looked back at his phone.

"When?" She wanted to know, her voice sharper now.

He didn't respond, the silence stretching uncomfortably between them.

"Lolu?"

He sighed and looked at her. "Don't start, Moyo!" His voice was low but firm, and then he looked back at his phone.

That was it. The indifference in his voice fanned the flames of her growing anger. "Don't start?!" She repeated, her voice rising as she glared at him. "So, wanting to spend time with you away from this house is 'starting' now? Is that it?"

Lolu set the phone aside, leaned back on the sofa, and sighed. "Moyo, I don't want to talk about this right now." He said with a frown on his face.

"Of course, you don't. It's always 'later' with you. Meanwhile, other families are making memories, going places, living life, doing whatever they need to do, and we're just ... here! Here!" She shot back, her arms flinging wide.

"Moyo, I said we'll go!" He did not shout but his tone was dismissive. "Can we leave it at that? Let's not argue this evening."

Her anger bubbled over, but she bit her lip, forcing herself to hold back the sharp words dancing on her tongue. Instead, she shook her head, hissed, and got up from the sofa.

As she walked out of the room, she muttered just loud enough for him to hear, "I knew that is what you would say. As always, no money. I can't believe this!"

He said nothing in response, and the silence frustrated her more.

In the bedroom, she sank onto the bed, staring at the ceiling as her emotions tangled between anger and disappointment.

The next morning, Monday, her feelings hadn't softened, and she left the house for work still upset. She wasn't happy, and she blamed Lolu for it.

During her lunch break, as she continued thinking, she remembered that someone in her church had said that people should do things that would make them happy.

Taking her phone, she decided to call James. She needed to make herself happy, she thought.

"Hi, James." She said, greeting him as soon as he picked up the call.

"Hey, Moyo,"

They exchanged greetings, and then she asked, "Are you free this Saturday?" She knew her husband had an event in church that day and wouldn't know her movement.

"This Saturday works. I have a meeting in my office in the afternoon. So, shall we say 6pm?" James wanted to know.

As she said *okay*, she told herself that she needed to make herself happy even if just for a moment; Lolu was not making her happy.

That Saturday, she told her mother that she needed to see someone, and she dropped her son off with her.

As she drove to the restaurant, she was thinking about James, excited. It was as if she was going to meet a man she loved, and her mind wandered to their past, to moments they had shared.

When she got there, she called James to find out where he was, and he said he was on his way. He had a little delay in the office.

She alighted from her car, entered the cozy restaurant, and chose a table by a window. While waiting, she looked around the restaurant, watching the gentle bustle of the evening crowd. After some minutes, she decided to use her phone and took it out.

About ten minutes after, James called to let her know he had arrived and was parking his car.

She put her phone down and watched the door so she could have a good look at him when he entered the large room. Within minutes, the door opened, and as he strode in with the same easy confidence she remembered, she looked at him. He looked the same—well-dressed and confident. This was someone who had once been such a big part of her life.

"Hey, Moyosore," he greeted her, a warm smile spreading across his face.

She stood, and he gave her a brief hug as they greeted.

She sat down, and as he slid into the seat across from her, he said, "It's been a while."

"Yeah, it has." Moyo replied, offering a soft smile as she nodded.

"You look good." There was that familiar glint of charm in his eyes as he spoke, still smiling.

"Thank you," she replied, returning the smile.

Moyo was in a soft, cream-colored dress. She had chosen something simple but elegant, hoping to keep things casual, yet polished. Her braids were neatly arranged into a stylish bun at the top of her head, secured with pins.

She complimented him on his dressing as well, and he thanked her.

He asked, "I hope you're not in a hurry to leave."

She smiled and shook her head. Her son was safely with her mother, and her husband was in church, so she was free to focus on this meeting.

"Good." He said.

They both ordered their drinks and the waiter left.

When James started talking, Moyo found herself listening more to the sound of his voice than his words. It felt strange to be here with him, to be sitting across from someone who had once been such a big part of her life. He hadn't changed much—still the same well-dressed, confident man who always knew how to make a lasting impression.

"So, how have you been?" He eventually said, breaking her thoughts.

Moyo paused for a moment before answering, trying to keep her emotions in check. "I've been good. And busy, you know, but life is steady."

James nodded, giving her an understanding look. "I can imagine. I'm glad to hear things are going well."

Moyo wasn't sure what this meeting would lead to, but for now, she'd let the conversation unfold.

"How about you?" She leaned back in her chair.

James gave a small shrug. "Busy, also. Work's been hectic. I'm juggling a lot, but it's good."

The waiter returned to serve their drinks.

Moyo blessed her drink and began to sip it slowly.

They continued talking, reminiscing about old times.

Soon, their food was served, and when he saw that she wanted to bless only her food, he asked her to bless everything on the table. She prayed briefly, and he said Amen.

They began to eat as they continued talking.

At one point, Moyo shifted the conversation to his business.

He leaned back in his chair, a glint of pride in his eyes as he spoke. "I've been busy with my business," he said, in a voice that had an edge of excitement. "Things have really taken off. I started a digital marketing agency a few years ago, and it's been growing faster than I had ever expected."

Moyo raised an eyebrow, intrigued. "That sounds impressive. How did you manage to get it off the ground?"

James grinned, clearly proud of his success. "It wasn't easy, at first. A lot of late nights and taking risks, but I had a vision. I wanted to create a business that didn't just make money but really helped clients grow their brands. We've worked with some major companies, a few luxury brands, and even some influencers who've seen a huge increase in engagement after working with us."

He paused, taking a sip of his drink before continuing. "The profits have been great. We've scaled up quickly, expanding our team, and investing in new tech. Honestly, I'm in a place now where I'm thinking about what's next— maybe branching out into international markets."

Moyo listened intently, impressed, despite herself. She had known James had a sharp mind but hearing him talk about his business like this reminded her of how ambitious he had always been.

"That's amazing, James," she said, genuinely impressed. "You always did know how to make things happen."

He chuckled. "I guess some things never change. But enough about me. What about you, Moyo? I'm sure you've been doing some interesting things yourself."

She told him she was doing well and said a little about her job.

"How's your spiritual life?" She asked, tilting her head. "Still going to church regularly?"

James's expression shifted, with a hint of sheepishness creeping into his eyes. "Not as much as I should, honestly. You know I'll tell you the truth. Work gets in the way. By the time Sunday comes around, I'm just too drained to go most weeks."

Moyo raised an eyebrow, her tone light but pointed. "Hmm, excuses. You know better than that, James."

He chuckled. "I know, I know. I need to get back on track."

"So, why aren't you married yet?" Moyo asked, curiosity getting the better of her.

James smiled, leaning back in his chair. "I just haven't found the right woman," he said simply.

Moyo nodded. Absentmindedly, she stirred her glass of lemonade as her thoughts lingered on his answer.

Soon, the conversation shifted to lighter topics, and she found herself laughing more than she had in weeks. But beneath the surface, a quiet unease stirred, reminding her of the choices she was making and the lines she was walking. She felt a little guilty.

James studied her for a moment, and then leaning forward slightly, he lowered his voice and said, "Moyosore," his tone was serious now. "Look, I still like you. A lot. I haven't been able to get you out of my mind all this time."

Moyo blinked, caught off guard by his directness. For a moment, the words hung between them, and then she burst into laughter, shaking her head. "James, go and marry." She said, her laughter ringing out in the small space.

He smiled faintly, but there was a tinge of sadness in his eyes. "You think I'm joking?"

"No, I know you're not." She said, her tone softening. "But James, we're not those people anymore. And I … I'm married."

He nodded slowly, his gaze dropping to the table. "Yeah, I know. I just ... I needed to say it."

"Well, now you've said it," she replied, her voice light but kind. "Now go and do something with your life. I'm sure you'll find someone who'll make you happy soon. And don't skip church." She chuckled to ease the tension.

"Alright, Moyo. You win." He said, holding up his hands in a gesture of surrender. "But can we remain friends and keep in touch?"

Moyo paused for a moment, then nodded. "Yes, sure." She replied. There should be no harm in that, surely, she told herself even though her heart fluttered a little at the idea of reconnecting with him.

After some minutes, she decided to ask about his family. "How's everyone at home?"

"They're all fine." James replied with a small smile. "Dad's still running his bread bakery business, and Mom … well, you know her—always busy with one thing or another."

Moyo nodded, then tilted her head. "And your sister? How's she doing?"

James's expression darkened slightly. "She's divorced."

Moyo's eyes widened in shock. "Divorced? What happened?"

The last she knew about James's sister, she seemed to have a happy marriage. She had a good job, and she had even supported her husband by giving him a large amount of money to start his business.

James sighed and leaned back in his chair. "Yeah, it's hard to believe. After her husband's business took off, he left her for a younger woman."

Moyo felt a chill run through her. "You're joking, right?"

"I wish I were." James said bitterly. "She gave everything to that man, helped him when he had nothing. And when he made it, he threw her away like she didn't matter."

Moyo sat back, her mind racing. A part of her ached for James's sister, but another part of her was alarmed. Could this happen to her too?

She had already started supporting her husband financially, but what if, after everything, she ended up empty-handed, just like James's sister? No, she couldn't let that happen to her. Maybe it was time to step back and do less, she decided.

They talked for a while longer, catching up on mutual acquaintances, and laughing about the past. The conversation flowed easily, as if no time had passed at all, despite the years of separation between them. When they were ready to leave, James took a picture of them together with his iPhone and forwarded it to her. Afterward, he settled the bill, leaving a generous tip for the waiter.

And that was how they began to call each other regularly, each conversation filled with updates and moments of laughter. They also chatted on WhatsApp, exchanging pictures and messages about anything and everything, as if they had never been apart. Though they kept the tone light, Moyo could feel a growing connection.

As her friendship with James deepened, her relationship with her husband reduced.

When Nancy and Adesua returned from their vacation in July, they told Moyo that they had brought gifts for her and would bring them when they visited for her birthday.

CHAPTER 6

LOLU'S SCHOOL WENT on vacation on July 9. He had signed up to teach during the break to earn extra money, and classes resumed a week later on Monday, July 19.

Moyo's birthday was on Saturday, and although Lolu wasn't happy with her at the moment, he still planned to buy her a gift. The previous day, the pastor had reminded the husbands in church about their responsibility to love their wives, while Christian wives should submit to their husbands. Despite Moyo not submitting to him, Lolu felt encouraged by the pastor's words to continue loving her. In addition to the gift, he also planned to make breakfast for her that day.

The next day, after leaving school, Lolu stopped by a store to buy a blouse, which he carefully wrapped as her gift.

On Saturday morning, after waking up, he prayed for Moyo. Once he got out of bed, he retrieved the small, wrapped gift from the closet and handed it to her.

"This is for you. Happy birthday." He said nicely and gave her a light peck which he knew felt empty.

****

Moyo thanked Lolu and took the gift from his hand, offering a polite smile that was equally devoid of excitement. Placing it beside her on the bed, she picked up her phone and began scrolling through the congratulatory messages.

Once he stepped into the bathroom, she unwrapped the gift and found a lilac blouse—her favorite color. It was beautiful, and she appreciated the gesture, yet it seemed not enough. *Just a blouse?*

Another thought crept into her mind—how much had it cost? Though she hadn't expected to find a price tag, she checked anyway, confirming its absence. With a sigh, she placed it in her closet and returned to bed.

As she resumed checking her messages, she debated whether to remind James that today was her birthday. On second thought, it didn't seem necessary. Perhaps she'd mention it in passing later.

Lolu soon returned to the bedroom. He dressed up and headed to the kitchen to prepare breakfast for her—boiled yam and egg sauce.

When Moyo stepped out to wake Jerry, she was taken aback by the enticing aroma drifting from the kitchen. Seeing Lolu busy cooking, she hesitated for a moment before continuing on to Jerry's room.

When the food was ready and the table was set, Lolu called her, and she went over with Jerry.

At about 11.30am, she was in the kitchen preparing fried rice for the friends and family who might stop by when her phone began to ring. To her surprise, it was James.

"Hey, Moyosore! Happy birthday!"

"Thank you." She replied, careful not to mention his name, in case Lolu could hear her.

Smiling, she spoke again, "So, you remember?"

"Of course I do." He said with a chuckle. "And I have a gift for you. I'll have it ready tomorrow. Why don't you come by my office on Monday or whenever you can, to pick it up?"

A gift? Moyo was surprised. "Okay, I'll come by on Tuesday."

The call lasted about seven minutes.

Around two in the afternoon, her mother arrived with Alfred and his wife. They presented her with gifts and spent some time chatting and laughing together.

Lolu captured moments of Moyo with her family, then handed his camera to Alfred so he could take a picture with her.

As they were getting ready to leave at four, Nancy and Adesua arrived, greeting everyone warmly before handing Moyo the gift bags they had brought.

Later, as they talked, Nancy mentioned that she would be attending a wedding the following Saturday, with the reception set to take place at Crystal Garden Hall.

When they were about to leave around six, Lolu took more pictures of Moyo with her friends, preserving the memories of the day. In the evening, he forwarded all the pictures to her phone.

On Tuesday, Moyo attended a case hearing in court. When it ended and she left at 2.35pm, she drove to James' office. This was her second visit there. The two-story building housed a restaurant on the ground floor, while James' office and an insurance company occupied the first floor.

James welcomed her with a bright smile, and handed her a small, neatly wrapped box.

As she carefully opened it with a mix of curiosity, guilt, and smile, he watched her with his own warm smile, waiting for her reaction.

She brought out the box, opened it, and her eyes widened in surprise. Inside was an expensive wristwatch, its face gleaming under the office lights. It was beautiful—far more than she would have expected from just a friend.

"This is expensive! How much did it cost?"

He chuckled. "Don't worry about it. It's a gift."

"I—I don't know if I should take this."

James looked at her intently. "I wanted to give you something special. You deserve it. No strings attached."

She hesitated. "Are you sure?"

He laughed. "I'm serious!"

"In that case, thank you, James. It's too much but thank you." She accepted the gift.

Looking pleased with himself, he asked, "So, how did you celebrate your birthday on Saturday? Anything special?"

Moyo shrugged. "Not really. My mom, my brother and his wife, and a few friends came over to the house. Other than that, it was a quiet day."

James raised an eyebrow. "Oh, good."

They didn't talk for some seconds, and then he spoke again, "I'm curious … how's marriage treating you?"

The question caught her off guard. She hesitated, but then said, "Can I confess the truth to you?"

He leaned forward and said in a gentle voice. "Of course, you can. You know you can tell me anything. We always did before."

Moyo opened her mouth, then closed it. The words felt stuck.

"Hold on," James said, breaking the silence. "Why don't we go to the restaurant downstairs, and we can talk while having lunch?"

She nodded, agreeing, and they headed down to the small, cozy restaurant. They sat down and ordered food.

The waiter brought water to them, and when he left, James started the conversation by asking about her husband.

"So, where does your husband work?" He asked casually.

Moyo made a sound before she said, "He teaches at a school and works as a photographer."

"Works as a photographer?"

She nodded.

"That's all he does?"

She nodded and took a sip of her water.

He didn't talk as he searched her face.

As Moyo put her cup down, she felt a need to share more and be understood. After all, this was James—someone who had known her well, someone who could understand her better than most.

She hesitated, then decided to say a little more about her marriage. "I've been asking him to look for a better job." She confessed, her voice lowering slightly. "Am I asking for too much?"

James shook his head. "No, not at all. It's not too much to want more for your family."

Moyo's heart felt lighter hearing his words.

The waiter returned with their food and left. Moyo blessed the food, and they began to eat.

James spoke, "I don't mean to be nosy, but can I know what he gave you for your birthday?"

"A blouse."

"Hmm."

As they continued eating, she discovered that she was sharing more about her marriage, about how she felt unfulfilled, how things had changed over time, and her fears about their finances.

"I'm sorry to hear that." James eventually said. "If you ever need my help with anything, don't hesitate to ask."

She smiled faintly, feeling both comforted and conflicted. "Thank you, James. I appreciate that."

When they finished eating, she left and returned to her office.

Being Tuesday, the apartment was empty when she returned home at 7.10pm, as Lolu had gone to church with Jerry.

At 8.30pm, she received a message from James on WhatsApp. It was short; just a question and her bank account details.

Do you still use this bank account?

Moyo responded.

Yes. Why?

He did not reply.

She was about to call him after she had waited for three minutes when her phone alerted her to a message. It was a bank credit alert, and when she checked, she saw a credit alert from her bank. James had transferred some money into her account.

Both surprised and happy, she immediately called him. "Why did you send me money?"

"I just wanted to help, Moyo." James replied. "If this can help in any way, I'm happy to do it."

Moyo was silent for a moment, overwhelmed by his generosity. "Thank you." She said, her voice full of gratitude. "You didn't have to, but thank you."

"You're welcome." James said. "I just want you to know I'm here for you."

Shortly after, the call ended, but thoughts about him did not end. Still smiling, Moyo began to process everything … the gift, the money, the conversation. It was all so unexpected. And yet, in some strange way, it felt like a reminder of the bond they had once shared.

As Moyo continued thinking, she wondered where this new path would lead.

When Lolu returned home at 9.45pm, he told Moyo that a member of his church would be getting married on Saturday, and he would want them to go together.

"Why do you want me to go with you?" She asked with a frown.

In a controlled voice, he explained that they hadn't gone out together in a while, and the distance between them seemed to be widening, which he felt was harmful to their marriage.

He said that the solemnisation would hold in the bride's church while the reception would be at a hall near the church. "I don't plan to attend the church service though, only the reception." He added, patiently.

"This Saturday?" There was a hint of questioning in her voice.

"Yes. Just the reception; it will be at the Crystal Garden Hall."

"Crystal Garden Hall?" She repeated, her brows furrowing in thought. "Hmm. That's where Nancy said she'd be attending a wedding reception this Saturday."

Lolu shrugged. "Could be the same one."

"What's your church member's name?"

"Ramsey."

Moyo grabbed her phone and dialed Nancy's number.

After a few rings, her friend picked up. "Hello, Moyo! What's up?"

"Hey, Nancy," Moyo said. "Quick question—are you still attending that wedding reception at Crystal Garden Hall on Saturday?"

"Yes, I am," Nancy answered.

"Is the groom's name Ramsey?"

"Yes. Why?"

"Well, it turns out he attends my husband's church." Moyo said, smiling, suddenly interested in attending the event.

"Oh, wow! I had no idea your husband knew Ramsey. It's such a small world."

"Is the groom the one you know or the bride?"

Nancy laughed. "Both of them are my friends."

Moyo told her that her husband had asked her to attend the reception with him.

"Good, I'll be seeing you on Saturday then." Nancy said.

Moyo's voice brimmed with excitement. "What's the color code? Do you know?"

"Orange on turquoise."

Moyo thought about it for some seconds, and then said, "Oh good, I have the colors."

After the call, Lolu said, "Nancy knows them?"

"Yes." She returned to the flat tone she typically used with her husband.

"Is she coming with her husband?" Lolu wanted to know.

"I don't know. I didn't ask her." Moyo answered.

That Saturday, Lolu and Moyo dressed up for the wedding. Moyo wore *iro* and *buba* that was turquoise blue while the headtie was orange, with matching accessories. Lolu looked sharp in white attire. Their son, Jerry, was also dressed for the occasion, wearing a nice shirt, red bow, and pants. The red bow made him look like a little gentleman.

At the right time, they left the house. Lolu was behind the wheel and as they drove to the venue and made small talk, he glanced at Moyo, and his eyes fell on her wristwatch.

"That's a nice watch." He said, his tone casual. "Where did you get it from?"

Moyo hesitated, her fingers brushing against the sleek band. "It was a birthday gift." She replied after a moment.

Lolu raised an eyebrow. "A birthday gift? You didn't tell me. From whom?"

"A friend."

"That's an expensive one." Lolu noted, his voice now carrying a hint of curiosity. "Which of your friends?"

"You don't know him." Moyo said quickly, keeping her gaze fixed on the road ahead.

"A *him*?" Lolu asked, his tone sharpening slightly.

"Yes," she replied, trying to sound nonchalant.

"What's his name?"

Moyo's heart raced. If she said "James," Lolu would instantly recognize the name of her ex. Thinking fast, she decided to give James' middle name, "Kunle."

Lolu gave her a sideways glance but didn't say anything further.

Moyo, meanwhile, focused on keeping her composure, and hoped that the topic wouldn't come up again.

They were almost at the reception venue when Moyo received a call from Nancy, who wanted to know where she was. Nancy was already at the reception but would be leaving soon as her husband had called to say their child had a fever. Moyo assured her they were almost there and asked where she was seated. Nancy replied that she was standing near the entrance, waiting for Moyo before leaving.

When they arrived and entered the hall, Moyo scanned the room and spotted Nancy walking toward them. They exchanged greetings, and then Nancy left.

With Lolu carrying Jerry, they made their way to a table occupied by just one person. After greeting the person, they took their seats. From their spot, they had a clear view of the newlyweds. The MC was speaking, and they listened attentively.

Within minutes, uniformed servers arrived at their table, serving food and drinks. Once they finished eating, they continued watching the ongoing activities.

A little while later, as Lolu scanned the hall, his eyes landed on a familiar face walking into the hall. His expression brightened, and he called out, "Pat!"

The gorgeously dressed beautiful lady paused and turned, searching for the source of the voice. When her eyes landed on Lolu, recognition dawned, and a wide smile spread across her face. She hurried over; her excitement evident. It had been years since she'd last seen him.

"Lolu! Oh my goodness, it's been ages!" Pat exclaimed, reaching out to hug him briefly.

"It really has, Pat." Lolu said, grinning. "I didn't expect to see you here. How have you been?"

"I've been great! And you?"

"I'm doing well. Let me introduce you to my wife." Lolu gestured toward Moyo, who smiled politely. "Moyo, this is Pat, an old friend from university. Pat, meet my wife, Moyo."

"It's lovely to meet you." Pat said warmly, extending her hand.

"Nice to meet you too." Moyo replied, shaking her hand.

Pat looked at Jerry who sat on the chair between Lolu and Moyo. "I guess this is your son."

"Yes." Lolu answered.

"Wow, he's so cute!"

She wanted to know his name and Lolu told her.

"Mind if I sit with you?" Pat asked and looked from Lolu to Moyo.

"Of course, sit," Lolu said, gesturing to one of the two empty chairs at the table.

Pat settled in, and when a server offered her food, she declined and asked for malt to drink.

"I ate not quite long ago." She announced.

She got the malt and as sipped her drink slowly, she and Lolu began to chat.

Moyo listened, and smiled at the right moments, but she couldn't help noticing the ease with which they talked. She occasionally chimed in.

Lolu wondered if Pat was married. He debated asking her directly but decided against it, not wanting to come across as nosy.

Instead, he smiled and asked, "So, Pat, how have you been?"

Pat leaned back in her chair; her expression relaxed. "I've been doing great, Lolu. I run my own business now. It keeps me busy, but I enjoy it."

"That's impressive." Lolu said genuinely. It was obvious that she was doing well. "What kind of business?"

"Event planning." She replied with a proud smile. "Weddings, parties, corporate events—you name it. It's a lot of work, but it's rewarding."

"That's amazing." He said, nodding. "You were involved in such things back in school."

Pat laughed. "True! What about you? What do you do these days? Hold on, let me guess—you're into photography."

Lolu laughed. "Yes, actually. You got it right. I'm teaching at a school too, but photography is my main hustle."

"Really?" Pat said, her eyes lighting up. "I'm proud of you. Wow! That's great, Lolu. Your work must be amazing."

"Thank you." He said, clearly pleased by her enthusiasm.

Pat leaned forward slightly. "Can I have your number? I'd love to call you sometime. I have a photographer that I use for my events, but I can bring you on board as well."

Lolu smiled, happy.

They exchanged numbers, Pat saving his contact with a quick tap on her phone.

She wanted to know if he was on Instagram and when he said yes, she got his name on it.

"I'll definitely reach out soon." She assured him.

As Lolu and Pat continued their conversation, Moyo sat quietly, observing them, with a polite smile and a mix of emotions she couldn't quite articulate. Lolu leaned slightly forward as he listened to Pat, and she noticed how happy he seemed—his smile broad, and his laughter genuine. He also looked undeniably handsome in his suit.

Her gaze shifted to Pat, who exuded a confident warmth and success. She had the feeling that Pat might like Lolu. There was an ease in the way she spoke to him, and a certain spark in her eyes as she talked with him.

When there was a lull in the conversation, Moyo seized the moment. "How's your family? Husband, children?" She asked Pat, her tone casual but laced with curiosity.

Pat shook her head, a faint smile on her lips. "No. I'm not yet married."

Lolu, intrigued, tilted his head slightly. "Why not?" As he looked at her, he thought she was still very beautiful.

Pat laughed, brushing a stray strand of hair behind her ear. "Well, I haven't met the right man yet. Besides, I've been focused on my business, I guess I just haven't had the time."

Lolu nodded, his gaze lingering on her for a moment longer than Moyo liked. "It will happen soon by God's grace, in Jesus' name." He prayed sincerely.

"Amen. Thanks, Lolu."

About twenty minutes after, it was time for Lolu and Moyo to leave.

As they gathered their things, Pat turned to them. "Did you come in your car?"

"Yes."

"Would you mind giving me a ride?" She asked. "Someone hit my car on Thursday, and it's still at the workshop, being repaired."

"Of course." Lolu said without hesitation, glancing at Moyo, who nodded in agreement.

Lolu carried Jerry, and they walked to the car together.

As Pat slid into the backseat, she looked around appreciatively. "This is a nice car." She said with a smile.

"Thank you," Lolu replied, glancing at her in the rearview mirror.

The drive was pleasant, with Pat sharing a few stories about their university days and cracking jokes that made Lolu laugh.

Moyo joined in occasionally but spent most of the ride in quiet reflection, acutely aware of the energy between her husband and Pat.

CHAPTER 7

WHEN THEY DROPPED Pat off at her home, she thanked them warmly. "I really appreciate the ride. It was so nice catching up, Lolu, and meeting you, Moyo."

"Same here." Moyo replied with a polite smile.

As they drove away, the atmosphere in the car shifted. Moyo glanced at Lolu, who seemed lost in thought, a small smile still playing on his lips. She wondered what he was thinking.

Her curiosity barely hidden behind her calm tone, she asked, "Who exactly is she?"

Surprised by the directness of her question, Lolu moved slightly in his seat, and adjusted his grip on the steering wheel. "She's an old friend from school." He said casually, his eyes fixed on the road ahead.

"And how did she know about your photography?" Moyo pressed, her voice laced with skepticism.

Lolu sighed, sensing the subtle edge in her tone. "Because we talked about it back then. We were close."

"How close?"

He glanced briefly at her, and then said, "Just friends."

"Hmm." Moyo nodded slowly, folding her arms.

The drive home was quiet except for the faint sound of the engine. But Moyo's mind was anything but silent, as it replayed the interaction with Pat, dissecting every glance, word, and smile. As a woman, she could sense when another woman had feelings for a man, and she got the impression that Pat liked Lolu.

At the dinner table at home much later, the tension resurfaced. The aroma of spicy jollof rice filled the air, but Moyo seemed more interested in picking apart Lolu's past than the meal before her.

"Are you sure you were not in a relationship with Pat in school?" She asked, her fork pausing mid-air.

"Moyo, how many times will you ask me this question? I've already told you that we were just friends. What's the problem?"

Moyo leaned back in her chair, her eyes narrowing slightly. "There was a way she was looking at you." She said, her tone measured but probing.

Lolu didn't respond for some seconds, and then he chuckled, shaking his head. "Women!" He said under his breath.

"Is it funny?" Moyo asked, her brows arching.

"Yes. I don't know why you're bothering yourself unnecessarily."

"I think she would want more. Did it ever come up when you were in school?"

Lolu hesitated, then shrugged. "Well, some of our friends said so, but we didn't think so. At least, I didn't." He knew that Pat liked him then.

"I think she likes you." Moyo said, her voice softer now but still insistent.

Lolu set his fork down and met her gaze squarely. "What can I do about that? If I wanted to contact her, I could have. I know some people who know her, but I didn't. And I married you. Shouldn't that tell you something?"

Moyo's lips pressed into a thin line as she absorbed his words. She glanced down at her plate, poking at the rice absentmindedly. "I wonder what she would say if she knew how much you're actually making from your photography business." She mused.

"It's a free world, she can say whatever she wants but that's not her business, is it? Besides, I'm still able to put money down for some things, Moyo." He said, sounding a little angry as he took his fork.

She glanced up at him, her expression unimpressed. "It's not enough, and you know that." She said, her voice sharper than she had intended. "She said we have a nice car. I wonder what she would say if she realized that it's not yours. People see you driving a good car, and they think it's yours."

Lolu froze, his fork hovering mid-air as the words struck him like a punch.

Slowly, he set the fork down on the plate and pushed back his chair, the screech of wood against tile breaking the silence. Without a word, he stood and headed toward the bedroom, his face contorted with anger.

Moyo watched him retreat to the bedroom and heard the door shut behind him. She knew she shouldn't have said that—it was cruel and uncalled for—but the words had slipped out in her frustration. She felt bad with guilt as she sat alone at the table.

She continued eating.

The sound of her phone ringing broke the silence. It was Nancy.

"Hello, Nancy," Moyo said, trying to sound normal.

"Hi, Moyo. Just wanted to check. When did you and your husband leave the wedding?" Nancy asked cheerfully.

Moyo answered.

"Well, I didn't get a chance to greet your husband properly … I was in a hurry to leave." Nancy said. "Is he there with you so I can say hello?"

"Er - no. He's in the bedroom."

"Can you take the phone to him?"

"Yes, er … actually, Nancy, we just had a quarrel."

Nancy's voice immediately turned serious. "What happened?"

Moyo hesitated but in the end, relayed the incident.

As Moyo recounted the exchange, Nancy's disappointment was palpable. "You shouldn't have said that, Moyo." She said firmly. "You know that would hurt him. Why would you even bring up the car?"

Before Moyo could respond, Nancy said, "Hold on. I need to add Adesua to this call."

Within a minute, Adesua's voice chimed in. "What's going on?"

"Adesua, you won't believe what Moyo said to her husband." Nancy began.

When Nancy explained the situation, Adesua's reaction was swift. "Moyo, that was wrong. You can't speak to your husband like that, no matter how frustrated you feel! You know how sensitive men can be about these things. You need to apologize."

"I know I shouldn't have said it; it just slipped out."

"You must have been thinking it." Adesua said.

Nancy's voice softened. "You need to call him, Moyo, and apologize. Don't let this fester."

Moyo nodded to herself. "Alright. Thanks."

The two friends urged Moyo to fix things quickly, and they ended the call by saying they'd reach out to Lolu directly.

A few moments later, Moyo heard Lolu's phone ringing in the bedroom, and soon, his low, muffled voice indicated he had answered.

She finished eating and took the used items to the kitchen.

Back in the living room, she could still hear Lolu's voice. When the call ended, she mustered the courage to face him. She stood and walked to the bedroom.

Lolu was lying in bed, scrolling on his phone. He looked up briefly but said nothing.

"Lolu, maybe I shouldn't have said what I did." She began.

Maybe?! He didn't respond.

"I apologize."

"Okay." He said without looking at her.

"Lolu?"

After a pause, he looked at her, "I accept your apology, Moyo, but I won't drive your car again." His expression was calm but resolute.

"Lolu -"

"It's fine, Moyo." He said, cutting her off. "Let's not talk about it anymore."

She returned to the living room.

****

About an hour after, Lolu got up and went to the kitchen to find something to eat.

In bed later, he was thinking about the day when Pat's face crept into his mind, uninvited. The memory of her words, her smile, her laugh, the way she had looked at him—it lingered longer than necessary. He eventually prayed and slept.

The morning sunlight streamed through the windows as Lolu sat at the edge of the bed, tying his shoelaces, getting ready to go to church. He'd planned to shake off the remembrance of the previous night's argument with Moyo and move on, but as he sat there, his thoughts betrayed him. How could she have said what she said to him? Did she love him at all?

Before long, another face came to his mind - Pat's. And as he drove to the church, he found himself thinking about her. He tried to stop it but the thought seemed to be persistent.

On his way back home in the afternoon when he found that he was still thinking of Pat, he shook his head and said, "I reject these thoughts in Jesus' name".

He tried to dispel the thoughts, but they clung stubbornly. He almost couldn't believe this. He had been very careful with women since he became a Christian. So, how did she manage to slip through the barriers into his mind like this?!

At home, he was still thinking of Pat.

You must not cheat on your wife again, Lolu, he counseled himself. He had to fight the temptation, but as determined as he was, the pull was still there. The thought of Pat was alluring and persistent, and it scared him.

Realizing he couldn't fight this on his own, he began to pray. "Lord, help me." He whispered. "I can't do this without You. You've changed me, and I don't want to go back to who I used to be. Strengthen me. Keep me faithful to You, and to my wife even if she does not deserve it. Guard my actions, my heart and my thoughts, in Jesus' name."

He felt better after the prayer. He knew the struggle wasn't over, and he knew the battle wasn't going to be won in a single moment, but he felt a renewed strength to resist the temptation. He would pray more and focus on God and His word until the thoughts of Pat faded away. He must remain committed to fighting for his marriage and his faith every day, he resolved.

Four days passed, and Lolu had nearly managed to put Pat out of his mind, focusing instead on God, his work, and his family.

But that Thursday evening, as he sat in the living room reading a book, his phone began to ring with the name 'Pat' flashed on the screen.

He hesitated for a moment before answering. "Hello, Pat." He said cautiously.

"Hey, Lolu! How's it going?" Pat's voice was warm and familiar, and Lolu couldn't help but feel a small tug of nostalgia.

"I'm good. How about you?"

"I'm doing well. Just wanted to say hi." She said, a light laugh following her words.

They spoke for a few minutes, exchanging pleasantries.

Before they hung up, Pat said, "By the way, I'm thinking about doing a photoshoot soon. I'll let you know when I'm ready, but I wanted to ask you, what are your charges for a session?"

Lolu gave her the details, trying to keep the conversation as brief and professional as possible.

"I'll send you the information whenever you're ready." He added.

"Thanks. I'll keep you posted." She said. "Take care. My regards to your wife."

"Take care." Lolu replied, ending the call.

He put the phone down and when he looked up, he saw Moyo standing in the bedroom's doorway, her arms crossed, and a look of suspicion on her face.

"Was that Pat?"

He said yes.

"Why did she call you?"

"Just to say hello."

Moyo raised an eyebrow, her expression skeptical. "Just to say hello?"

Lolu sighed, setting his phone down. "Yes, and she said she'd like to do a photoshoot soon." He paused, realizing that his words probably hadn't done much to ease her concerns. "I've told you before, Moyo. There's nothing to worry about."

Moyo stood still for a moment, her gaze locked on him. He could see the doubt in her eyes, but he didn't talk as he took his book and continued reading.

It was on Tuesday when Pat called Lolu again. He had just closed from school and was walking to his car. She told him that she would be going on a business trip for a week, but when she returned, she would like to have a photoshoot at her house.

"In your house?" Lolu repeated, surprised by the request.

"Yes," Pat responded, her tone matter-of-factly. "I need to see your work up close. I'm thinking of giving you two event jobs if I like what I see."

Lolu thought for a moment. "I've got photos on my Instagram and Facebook. You can check those out."

"I already did," she replied quickly. "I want to see the work in person, Lolu. It's different, you know?"

He sensed a check in his spirit not to go to her house. There was something in the way she said it that triggered an uneasy feeling in his spirit. He had learned over time to listen to those little checks, but this time, the pull toward the job—the potential opportunity—was strong.

I need the money she will pay for the photoshoot, he thought. He had bills to pay, and he needed every opportunity that came his way. Besides, Pat seemed to be doing well and well-connected; she would be able to introduce him to her circle of friends.

"Okay. Day and time?"

They fixed Wednesday, August 25, at 2pm.

At home, he told Moyo about it.

"At her house?"

"Yes. It's purely business, Moyo." He pointed out. "And I'm going to be careful."

She shrugged and as she walked away, she said, "That's your business."

She had been thinking that talking to James without her husband's knowledge might not be right, but now that Lolu was talking to Pat, and would be going to her house, she guessed there was nothing wrong with her talking to James.

****

In the evening of Monday, August 16, James called Moyo, as he often did. Their conversations had become more frequent and more comfortable, and Moyo looked forward to them. James had a way of making her feel understood, and he had money, unlike Lolu.

Moyo and James had spoken about her plot of land before, but that day, James had a suggestion that made her pause.

"You should start developing it." He said, his voice encouraging. "Don't just let it sit there. If you don't develop it, you will spend the money on something else sooner or later. And if you keep it in a bank, it will be losing value. It's a great opportunity."

Moyo hesitated for a moment as her eyes went to the framed photo of Lolu on the bedroom wall. She wasn't sure how he would react. Having a land he was not aware of was one thing, but going ahead to build on it was another thing.

"I don't know. Lolu doesn't even know about the land yet. He'll be very upset." She revealed.

"Then tell him."

"I don't want to tell him yet."

"I understand." James said. "In that case, I think you should start developing it. When the house is built and you show him, he won't mind, after all, you're doing it for the family."

When she hesitated, he added, "You're not doing anything wrong. It's your investment after all."

Moyo considered his words. He was right in a way; it was her land, and her money. If she didn't do something with the money in her savings, she would spend it on other things. Besides, if she didn't do this, they might not have a house at all.

She nodded.

He spoke again. "Don't be like my sister who spent all her money on her husband, and was left with nothing."

"I think you're right." She decided she would go ahead. "But where do I start from?"

James, ever the pragmatic one, continued, "I told you that I'm almost done with my own house. I've got a great project manager. You could use him, Moyo. I trust him completely. He's helped me with everything."

Moyo wasn't one to easily trust others with big decisions, but James always seemed to know what he was doing, and his words were very convincing.

"Okay, I will, if you trust him and think I can use him." She finally said.

"I do, absolutely. I don't think I've shown you the pictures of my house, have I?"

"No."

"I'll send some pictures to you now. The man has done a fantastic job." He said. "I'm telling you; you'll be in good hands."

Within thirty seconds, four pictures dropped on her phone. She checked them and said she was impressed.

She told him the location of the land and agreed to meet him and his project manager at the site on Thursday afternoon.

That day, the three of them stood in front of the land, and James introduced the project manager to Moyo.

The project manager, a middle-aged man with sharp eyes and a professional demeanor, greeted Moyo with a firm handshake. And without wasting time, they began to discuss the project.

Moyo looked at the plot in front of her, the ground was bare but full of potential. She could picture the four-bedroom house she would like to build—spacious with bright colors. The plan seemed simple, but she knew it would take a lot of work and money.

James, who stood by her side, listened to her conversation with the project manager with approval, and gave his opinion where necessary.

As they walked around the site, discussing the potential design and timeline, Moyo felt a strange mix of excitement and guilt. The more they spoke, the more she imagined what her life could look like in this house. At the same time, she couldn't help but feel that this step she was taking might cause troubles in her marriage. Lolu was not aware she bought the land, and now, with James and the project manager involved, it felt like it might be too late to turn back.

She pushed those feelings aside however. She had always been determined, and now that she had a plan to build a house, she was going to follow through. If she didn't spend her money on this, it would eventually be spent on something else. Maybe once the house was built without her collecting money from him, Lolu wouldn't be upset much. It would be her investment, not his. Surely, he would understand and forgive her.

"I'd like a good job, please." Moyo appealed to the man when they were about to leave the site.

"Don't worry. We'll make sure everything goes smoothly." He assured her.

They left and while walking back to their cars, James told her, "Trust me, Moyo, this is going to be great. Once you get started, everything will fall into place."

The following Tuesday, Moyo, James, and the project manager were at the site again, and they agreed to start work immediately.

****

The next day—Wednesday—Lolu drove to Pat's house in his own car.

Pat was standing outside the beautiful house, talking to a teenage girl who was selling corn. When she saw the car and realized it was him, she called out to a man to open the gate.

Lolu drove inside the compound, got out of his car, and stood beside it.

She soon dismissed the girl selling corn and returned inside. Lolu carried his equipment and as they walked toward her apartment, she wanted to know whose car that was.

"This is my car. The one I drove that day is my wife's." He explained.

"Oh, I see."

They continued talking, and he admitted that things had not been easy for him. Inside her apartment, they continued talking, and he revealed that it had crossed his mind a few times to relocate abroad and start afresh.

She offered to help him financially, but he turned it down.

"I'll be fine." He said.

Soon, he began to get his camera and equipment ready, and she went into her room to dress up.

The photoshoot went smoothly, just like any other session. Pat was pleasant to work with, and her easygoing attitude made the time pass quickly.

When they finished, Pat asked for his bank account details, and paid for his service.

Then she surprised him. "I've prepared food for you."

Food. He hadn't eaten much all day. He felt a surge of temptation, but a sense of caution crept over him. *What if something goes wrong?* He thought. *This could lead to trouble.* He was married, and a Christian.

He declined. "No, thank you. I'll eat when I get home."

"I've already prepared it. Hold on."

She opened the kitchen door, stepped inside, and soon returned with a tray of food. Placing it on the table, she gestured toward it and said, "Take a look. I even have stockfish!"

Stockfish?! Is she serious? He looked at the table, and when he saw the food, he changed his mind. There might not even be much food at home, he thought.

"I will eat from it so you can know it's not poisoned." She added and chuckled.

He smiled. While he knew the situation was risky, he reasoned that it wouldn't hurt if he was careful. He checked the time; he still had some minutes before he needed to leave to pick up Jerry. He sighed. Maybe just this once wouldn't hurt.

"Okay." He said.

She looked pleased. "Good. Please, come over." She pulled out a seat for him at the table.

"Thanks." He said, sitting down.

She sat on the other side of the table, and said, "I'll serve you."

She did and then served her own food.

As they began to eat in silence for a few minutes, Lolu felt that the atmosphere between them had changed. *What am I doing?* He couldn't quite shake the nagging feeling that something was off. Still, he pushed it aside.

When they finished eating, he thanked her and got up to leave.

Pat stood and moved toward him, her eyes now intense with something more than friendliness.

"Lolu," she said softly, her hand reaching for his.

He stepped back.

She smiled. "It's okay."

"No, Pat -"

Before he could say more, she came closer, and he saw her lips pressing toward his. The moment felt suffocating, charged with an energy that made his pulse race.

He jerked back, heart pounding in his chest. "No!" He said firmly. "It's not right!"

Pat looked at him, her eyes filled with both surprise and challenge. "Lolu, don't be like that. It's just a kiss. It doesn't mean anything."

He shook his head and repeated, "No, it's not right."

"Everyone does it."

"Not everyone. I'm not doing it!"

Her eyes searched his as she said, "I've always liked you, Lolu. Er … your wife doesn't need to know about this."

"Pat, what you're suggesting is wrong, and I'm not going to compromise my faith and values for anything."

He turned, carried his bag, and as he headed for the door, she didn't try to stop him. He left the house quickly, his mind racing. As he walked to his car, part of him felt relief.

But another part wondered at his restraint. *I could've done it,* he thought. *I could've hurt Moyo like she's been hurting me. She's been distant and cold, and I could have done something to make her feel what I've been feeling.*

But even as the thought crossed his mind, he knew it wasn't from God, and yielding to sin wasn't the right thing to do. Moyo had her flaws, but he shouldn't cheat on her; he shouldn't sink to that level. If he cheated on her, he would not only be sinning against her, he would also be sinning against God.

No matter how tempting the sin was, he knew that he had made the right choice by saying no to it.

 CHAPTER 8

ON THE WAY home, Lolu kept replaying the events in his head—Pat's smile, and the way she had tried to pull him into her world.

As his thoughts swirled, a realization dawned on him. *It really is easy for married men to stray,* he thought. The world was full of women who didn't care if a man was married; women who were willing to share men. The temptation was everywhere, even in church, and the excuses to cheat were easy to find.

He exhaled sharply. A man had to be prayerful, determined and firm, if he wanted to do the right thing. Otherwise, he'd be swept away, with his marriage destroyed, and his vows broken. He knew this too well.

His thoughts turned to the man he used to be—before he became a Christian. Back then, he hadn't seen a problem with entertaining those temptations. He had been selfish and careless, and he had hurt people, including himself. But now, everything was different. He had given his life to Christ, and with that came a new standard; a new responsibility that he must keep honoring.

He knew he should discuss it with Moyo, and he would have loved to, but he didn't think he should. He didn't think she would understand as she seemed distant and lost in her own world lately.

****

On Saturday, Moyo, James, and the project manager were back at the site. It was early in the morning, and the team was full of anticipation, but as they started to go over the plans, two men appeared at the edge of the land, walking toward them with purpose.

Moyo had been talking, but she paused and squinted at the unfamiliar figures. The men didn't seem to belong to the area, and there was something intimidating about their presence.

The two men reached them, and one of them, a tall and broad-shouldered figure, spoke first. "Excuse me, but this land belongs to our family. We're asking you to leave." He said firmly, his voice low and threatening.

Moyo was surprised but she stood her ground. She would not be intimidated by them. "I paid for this land." She replied. "I bought it from Pa Jeremiah. He's the one who sold it to me."

The other man, shorter but no less imposing, shook his head. "Well, you'd better go and collect your money from him. This is family land, and you have no right to be here. We're telling you to stay away from this place."

Moyo glanced at James, who was standing beside her. She spoke again, "This land is mine. I have all the legal papers, the receipts, and the contracts. I've paid for it. You know Pa Jeremiah, don't you?"

The two men exchanged glances, then as they turned to leave, the tall man said, "We've warned you. Don't come here again."

With that, they walked away and soon disappeared into the distance.

Shocked, Moyo stood frozen, and it felt like the ground beneath her was shifting. "What was that about?"

James asked some questions about how she got the land, and she explained.

The project manager could sense her unease. "Don't worry, Madam. This is likely some kind of misunderstanding. Let's go talk to Pa Jeremiah, to sort it out. He'll clear everything up."

James nodded in agreement. "Yes. Let's get to the bottom of this before we make any decision."

Moyo agreed, and they all made their way to the house of the man who had sold her the land. Pa Jeremiah's house was a simple building not too far from the place.

When they explained what had happened, the man's face softened into a reassuring smile. "There's no cause for alarm." He said, leaning back in his chair. "Those two men are troublemakers. They're distant relatives, always looking for a fight, always trying to stir things up. The land has been sold to you, and everything is in order. I have the papers to prove it."

Moyo felt relieved, but the nagging doubts lingered. "Are you sure? They were so adamant. I don't want any problems down the line."

Pa Jeremiah chuckled. "I've dealt with them before. They like to claim things that don't belong to them, but don't worry. You're the rightful owner. The land is yours. Continue with your work."

Reassured, Moyo and the team decided to move forward with the project.

Over the next few weeks, they visited the site about five more times, making progress with the plans. Moyo released some money to the project manager who hired some people to clear the land, and soon they began to lay the foundation.

But every time they arrived, Moyo's eyes darted around, scanning her surroundings. She felt as if those two men could be lurking nearby as their angry faces still haunted her memory.

****

School resumed on Monday, September 20, and Lolu was there to teach another class of students.

The next day he received a call from Pat. Three weeks had passed since the confrontation with her.

Aware of the tension between them, he answered cautiously. "Hello."

"Hello, Lolu," Pat greeted him, her voice as smooth as ever.

"Pat, how are you?"

"I'm okay. Trying to keep body and soul together." She replied.

"Good."

When she didn't hear any more from him, she said, "I need to talk to you about something. It's a business proposal,"

Lolu's guard went up instantly. "A business proposal?"

"Yes."

"Okay. I'm all ears."

"No, it's not something I can explain over the phone. It's better we meet," she insisted, sensing his hesitation. "And don't worry, I'm not going to do anything. You've made yourself clear."

"I'm not coming to your house, Pat. If we need to see, then it will have to be somewhere public."

"That's fine." She agreed.

Lolu hesitated for a moment, and then he gave her his church address.

She was surprised. "Your church?"

"Yes. Since it's to discuss a business proposal, we can sit on a side in the church compound."

"Okay. I won't want to get down from my car though. We can discuss inside my car." She said.

That was fine with him, and they agreed on a time.

That day, he got to church early, and sat down, praying in tongues. Soon, Pat arrived in her car. She parked in the parking area, and he went to her. As he greeted her, he looked her over …she looked calm and composed.

"Thanks for meeting me." She said, her eyes scanning the area as if ensuring they were alone and there was no one that might be listening to their conversation.

"So, what's this proposal?" Lolu asked without wasting time. He wanted to keep the conversation focused on business.

Pat smiled, and after a moment, she spoke. "I'm going to Australia soon."

"Australia?" Lolu repeated, confused.

"Yes."

"Okay ... and how does that involve me?"

Pat's smile widened as she leaned in closer, lowering her voice just enough for him to feel the weight of her words. "Well, this is actually to help you."

"Help me? How?"

"You told me the day you came to my house that you wouldn't mind traveling abroad." She said.

He listened, wondering where this was leading.

She continued, "Let me explain what I have in mind before you respond."

"Okay."

Then she said, "We can travel together as a couple."

"As a couple?!"

"Listen, Lolu,"

Lolu stared at her, trying to process what she was suggesting.

She went on. "Once we settle down in Australia, you could divorce me, and then you can bring Moyo and your son over. It's a way for you to get out of the country and start afresh."

Lolu's heart raced. This was not the kind of proposal he was expecting. He felt a knot form in his stomach. *This is wrong.*

He had been tempted before, but this felt like a blatant attack on everything he stood for. It would complicate his life and could destroy his divine destiny.

He shook his head. "I can't do that, Pat. That's not a plan I can get involved in."

Pat's expression softened, almost as if she was trying to explain something to a child. "Listen, if you travel and things improve for you, it will help your family."

"Traveling might help, but this plan will destroy my family and my relationship with God. I won't be a part of it."

She looked at him, eyes narrowing slightly. "Are you saying this because you're a Christian?"

"Yes." He said without hesitation.

"But some Christians do these things." She said and mentioned a person she knew who claimed to be a Christian and had done something similar.

"Some professing Christians might do it, but that doesn't make it right. God determines what is right, not people. This is definitely not His plan for me, and it's not His plan for you."

Pat leaned back slightly, a faint smile tugging at the corners of her lips. "Okay, let's talk about your business then."

Lolu shook his head. "No, let's talk about you. You need to stop living like this, Pat. What you're suggesting is not the way to live. You need to know God and put your trust in Him. Are you so desperate to get married?"

When she sighed and looked away, he began to tell her that God loved her. Then he asked if she'd like to give her life to Jesus, but she shook her head and said she was already a Christian, just not a strong one.

Lolu sighed and said, "I'll be praying for you."

When he opened the door of her car, she asked, "Are you leaving?"

"Yes, I have to leave. Is there anything else?"

She shook her head, her eyes avoiding his as she spoke. "No, that's all."

He prayed briefly that the Lord would protect and lead her, and then he got out of the car.

"Bye, Lolu."

"Bye."

Without another word, he closed the passenger door and moved away from the car.

She started the car, and as she pulled away, she did not glance at him.

He turned and walked away, shaking his head in disbelief at her suggestion. He had done the right thing. It hadn't been easy, but he was glad he pleased God. Her suggestion would definitely complicate his life and grieve the Holy Spirit.

He decided that if she should contact him again, he would not answer it, and if he must talk to her, his wife must be involved. No *more chats, and no more visits without Moyo being around.* He was finished with the temptation; finished with the confusion. He must remain focused on his marriage, his family, and his walk with God.

****

The last day of September, Thursday, Moyo, James, and the project manager met on the site again. The workmen hired by the project manager did not come that day.

That afternoon, Moyo stood on the plot of land, inspecting the progress of the project, with James by her side. Pointing at the skeletal framework of the building, the project manager was explaining the works done by his workmen, and the changes that would have to be made to the design.

At a side of the land, James noted the bricks used. "These bricks here," he pointed, "you will need to replace them. They're not the quality we agreed on."

Moyo sighed, pulling her sunglasses which had been hanging on her head, over her eyes.

"We will get it fixed." The project manager agreed and explained what happened.

"Please monitor the workers, so that this project does not drag on." James told him.

Suddenly, the sound of shouting reached them, and they looked in the direction.

Five men, rough-looking and armed with sticks and machetes, approached quickly.

"Who gave you permission to build here?" One of the men barked.

The project manager stepped back quickly.

James stepped forward and raised a hand to stop them. "Gentlemen, please calm down."

"I said who gave you permission?"

James answered again. "We have all the legal documents. This land belongs to her." He pointed at Moyo.

But the men weren't interested in explanations, and one of them lunged at James, striking him on the shoulder with a stick.

The project manager ran away.

James wanted to run, but one of the men grabbed him and the other man continued hitting him with the stick. He fell down.

Moyo began to scream as she ran away. "Help! Somebody help us!"

But help did not come as one of the men pursued her. He soon caught up with her and began to hit her with a stick, and she also fell down as he continued hitting her.

****

Lolu had just picked up Jerry from the preschool that Thursday afternoon and was driving out of the school compound when he received a call from Moyo's brother.

"Ah, Alfred, good afternoon." He greeted.

"Good afternoon. Where are you?"

"I'm on my way home." Lolu answered.

"Are you okay?" Alfred asked.

As Lolu said yes, he wondered what kind of question that was.

"What about Moyo? Is she okay?" Alfred asked.

"She's fine, and at work." Lolu said. He thought Alfred's voice sounded panicky, and he hoped something bad had not happened to Moyo's mother.

"At work?! What's going on?!" Alfred asked. "My mother said someone called her a few minutes ago, to say that Moyo and her husband were attacked and seriously injured."

Lolu laughed. "Moyo and her husband? That's clearly not true."

"I thought so too. When my mother said so, I told her I doubted it because I saw your post on Instagram about twenty minutes ago."

"Yes." Lolu said. "You can call Mommy back and assure her that we are fine."

"Okay. I'd like to call Moyo as well, though. My mother would ask me if I heard Moyo's voice. You know how mothers are."

They laughed.

"I'll talk to you later. Take care." Alfred told him.

"You do the same. Thanks for calling." Lolu responded, and the call ended.

Within six minutes, Lolu's phone started ringing again. It was Alfred and he answered it. "Hello?"

"I called Moyo's phone and it was a stranger that picked it! The person said they are trying to take her and the man with her to a hospital."

"Wha-t?!" Lolu exclaimed.

Alfred went on. "The person said that Moyo and the man came to check their building project when they were attacked."

Lolu immediately slowed down the car, and then pulled into a store's parking lot so he could listen and understand what Alfred was saying. "Building project?! What building project?"

Alfred hesitated, sensing trouble.

"Building project?" Lolu repeated, his voice sharp. "What building project are you talking about, Alfred? Where did you hear this?"

Alfred was in his office, and he shifted uneasily in his seat. He hadn't expected the news to cause this kind of reaction from Lolu. "I—I don't know the full details. The person didn't go into specifics. They just mentioned that Moyo and the man went there to check on the progress of a building project, and they were attacked."

Lolu's mind raced. He couldn't process what Alfred was saying. *Moyo? A building project?* Moyo had never mentioned any building project to him. He thought he knew everything about her plans.

"Who told you this? Where did this happen? And who's the 'man'?"

"I don't know. The person must be confused because he said Moyo and her husband."

Lolu was feeling confused himself, and gripping the steering wheel tightly, he exhaled slowly, trying to calm himself. This wasn't making any sense.

He spoke again. "Where exactly did this happen? Can you get me a location?"

"I—uh, I think it was near the outskirts of town." Alfred said. "Somewhere off the main road. But I can't say for sure. I'll call her phone again to get more information from the person."

"I'll find out for myself." Lolu said and ended the call.

He called Moyo's phone right away and when a woman answered it, he wanted to know where Moyo was. The woman answered the question and gave him the address. She asked Lolu to come immediately as the hospital would need some deposit, and he said he would be on his way right away. The money he was paid for a job on Saturday was still in his bank account, and he decided it could be used.

Lolu called his mother to know if she was at home, and when she said yes, he said he'd be bringing Jerry over soon.

He slammed the car into drive, and with a swift movement, he accelerated out of the parking lot. As the car roared down the road toward his parents' house, his mind was racing, piecing together fragments of information. What was Moyo hiding? What was the building project about? And who was the man with her? The more he thought about it, the more the questions gnawed at him. He needed answers, and he would make sure he got them.

Soon, he reached his parents' house and went inside with Jerry. Not wanting to say much since he didn't know what exactly was going on, he simply told his parents that he had to go somewhere.

When he left the house, he called Alfred to let him know he was on his way to the place. Alfred asked for the address so he could join him, and he gave it to him.

After the call, he called Moyo's phone again so he could get more information. The same female voice picked it and confirmed that Moyo and a man came to check their building project.

What's going on?! Lolu wondered, but to the woman, he said, "Okay, thank you. I'll be there shortly."

He reached the hospital, and the female nurse at the front desk confirmed that Moyo was there.

"May I know who you are, sir?"

"I'm her husband." He said and glanced around the area; it looked clean.

When the nurse told him how much deposit he would pay for her treatment, he said he would like to see her first to confirm she was the one before paying.

The nurse considered the request reasonable, so she called another nurse and asked her to escort Lolu to Moyo's room.

Two female patients occupied the room—one asleep, the other awake. The nurse gestured toward the sleeping figure. Even before approaching, Lolu knew it was Moyo.

"Is she sleeping?" He asked.

The nurse said yes and explained that the doctor had attended to her and given her an injection to make her sleep.

Lolu could see bruises on her face, hands, and legs, and her clothes were dirty.

They returned to the front desk where Lolu paid the requested money. Moyo's phone had been given to the nurse, and she gave it to Lolu. The nurse explained that the project manager was at the site with Moyo, but ran away, unhurt. He returned only after the thugs had left, picked Moyo's handbag, and brought it to the hospital.

"Where's the bag now?" Lolu wanted to know.

"It's inside the cabinet by her bed."

He got the phone number of the manager and called him to get more information. Suspecting that there was more to the matter at hand, and if he told the man that he was Moyo's husband, he might not get the right answers to his questions, he simply said that he was a family member.

The manager said Moyo's car was still at the site, but the thugs had broken the windows.

Lolu asked for the name of the man with Moyo. When the manager said 'Mr. James,' Lolu immediately wanted to know his last name. The answer stunned him. Wasn't that Moyo's ex?! He would need to confirm with Moyo's brother. What was going on?!

Lolu returned to the room where Moyo was, and sat on the chair by her bed. He called Alfred to let him know he had reached the hospital.

"How is she?" Alfred asked, his tone filled with concern.

"She's sleeping," Lolu replied, his voice flat. "I've paid the deposit. The nurse said she was given an injection to help her rest."

Alfred said he had informed his mother, and they would be on their way soon.

Then Lolu asked, "Who is James Aku?"

"James Aku? That's Moyo's ex." Alfred answered. "What about him?"

"I just wanted to confirm." Lolu said. "I'll be expecting you."

Afterward, Lolu brought out Moyo's handbag from the cabinet, opened it and checked to see if anything might be missing. He didn't think so as her iPad and wallet were there.

He put the handbag back in the cabinet, and with her phone in his hand, he stepped out into the hallway. If some things were going on, her phone would hold some answers, he was certain.

Standing on one side, he opened WhatsApp on her phone, and searched for the name, James. He began scrolling through Moyo's chats with James, and the things he saw shocked him. There were pictures of the site under construction, taken from different angles. The project seemed to be in full swing.

But it wasn't just the pictures that froze him. It was the messages that followed. Conversations between Moyo and James, laughing, making plans, discussing the next steps of the project, and James telling her he loved her. There was undeniable intimacy in their exchanges; an unspoken closeness that made Lolu's blood boil. The most unsettling was the image of Moyo and James at a restaurant, their smiles too familiar; too comfortable.

He opened her e-mail inbox, and his heart sank when he saw the details of her salary. There were also some substantial amounts that she hadn't mentioned, and a secret savings account. He continued scrolling, with the feeling of betrayal growing.

Lolu's heart raced as he quickly forwarded everything to his phone; his hands were almost shaking as he did so. His mind was a whirlwind of thoughts, all centering on one burning question: *What was going on between Moyo and James?*

His mind immediately gave an answer – Moyo was cheating on him. Was that possible? Moyo—a married woman! He wondered. As he thought about this, he remembered a married woman with three children in his former office who was having an affair with one of the managers.

He had no idea how far this had gone, when it started, or what Moyo had been hiding, but he knew he needed to confront her as soon as she woke up.

Back in the room, he glanced at her sleeping form. He had thought he knew her, and that he knew what she could do and not do. He had thought she was a Christian. Now, it all seemed like a lie. His trust in her was shattered, and he had no idea how to piece it back together.

 CHAPTER 9

STILL REELING FROM the shock, Lolu went to the hallway again and called Adesua. He needed to know if she was aware of these things that Moyo did. Fortunately, she picked the call.

"How are you?" Adesua asked pleasantly.

"I'm in shock."

Adesua was surprised at the response. "Why?"

He answered with a question. "Did you know that my wife has been seeing James?"

There was a pause on the other end of the line. "James? As in … your wife's ex?"

"Yes."

"Well, she told me she saw him in a bank some months ago, and then another time in traffic. That was all. What do you mean by she has been seeing him?"

Instead of answering her question, he said, "I have another question. Did she tell you that she bought a land and had started building on it?"

"Building on it?! Tell me you're joking!"

"I wish I were."

"You mean she's building on the land, and you were not aware?" Adesua found it difficult to believe.

"Yes, and I'm just getting to know about everything today."

"Please back up, I don't seem to understand all these things you're telling me." Adesua said. "Where did you get this information from?"

"She's in a hospital now."

"What?!" Adesua exclaimed. "What happened to her?"

"James is also here." He added.

Adesua exclaimed again. "What is James doing there?"

As Lolu explained what had happened to Moyo, Adesua exclaimed again and again. Afterward, she said she was preparing for her TV show and would not be able to come over that evening but would definitely see Moyo the next day to confirm all that Lolu had told her. She also promised to call Nancy, to inform her.

When the call ended, he returned to the room and sat on the chair by her bed. How could Moyo do this to him? To their marriage? As he went through the messages again, he thought of everything he had known about Moyo up until this point, and their marriage. Now, their marriage felt like a house of cards, ready to collapse with a single push.

Did her family members know that she had reconnected with James? Needing answers, he decided to check her chats with her mother.

While scrolling through the chats, he discovered that Moyo gave her mother lace fabric and a phone handset but gave his mother Ankara against her mother's counsel. He became more upset. Did she love him at all?

He put her phone inside her handbag and waited for the arrival of her mother and brother.

When they came, he greeted them and got up from the chair so that Moyo's mother could sit.

They wanted to know what the doctor had said, and how she was, and he answered them.

And then he began to tell them about some of the things he had discovered. They were shocked.

"She's been hiding things from me. And she has apparently hooked up with her ex, James."

"James?!" Moyo's brother and mother asked in unison.

"Yes. He was the one with her when it happened. He's the one she's been working with on the building project. Look at this!" He said, and showed them a picture.

Moyo's mother's face fell.

He showed them more pictures.

"Why would she do this? I just don't understand." Moyo's mother finally said.

"I need to get to the bottom of this." Lolu announced.

"Yes, you have to, but right now, you need to stay calm." She counseled him.

Alfred said they would need to report the incident to the police. "Where's Moyo's car now?"

"It's still at the site. I learned those men have broken the windows."

"We will need to get her car from there."

Lolu shook his head. "I'm not reporting this to the police, and I'm not dealing with her car. She never told me she was coming here, so I'm not getting involved. If this hadn't happened, I wouldn't have even known she was here. She would have gone home and pretended she was at the office all day. Do you know how many times she's been here without telling me?"

Moyo's mother sighed. "I almost can't believe she did this."

"So, where's James now? Is he in this same hospital?" Alfred asked.

"That reminds me. I'd like to see him if he is here." Lolu stated.

"I'll go with you." Alfred said immediately.

"Please be careful. Let's handle this with wisdom. Don't say anything to him; don't quarrel with him." Moyo's mother counseled Lolu.

At the reception, Lolu asked to see James, and he was directed to the room. There, a man was standing by James' bed, talking with him.

"Is that him?" Lolu asked Alfred.

"Yes."

As they approached James' bed, he and the man looked at them.

"I am Moyo's husband." Lolu announced. "So, you were with my wife!"

Alfred took Lolu's hand to calm him. "It's okay. Let's go."

Lolu decided to listen to Alfred so he would not do something he would regret. Without another word, he left with Alfred.

In the hallway, he headed in the direction of the front door.

Alfred followed him. "Where are you going?"

"I need to understand what exactly happened. I'd like to see the site of the project and also get more information."

Alfred called his mother's phone and told her he was going to the site with Lolu, and they would be back soon.

As they walked toward the front door, they talked while Alfred continued to express his shock.

Once inside Alfred's car, they headed to the site. Lolu didn't move around when they arrived; instead, he stood in front of the site, taking pictures, while Alfred captured images of Moyo and James' cars.

Lolu spoke with three residents from the house across the site, gathering what they knew. Afterward, Alfred told one of the men that someone would come the next day to retrieve Moyo's car, and he exchanged phone numbers with the man.

From there, Alfred drove to the nearest police station to file a complaint.

On the way back to the hospital, he advised Lolu to stay calm and recognize that this was a satanic attack against his marriage.

Back in the hospital, they found Moyo was still sleeping.

Shortly after, a nurse came to attend to Moyo. When she was leaving, Alfred asked how James was faring, and when both James and Moyo would be discharged.

"Mr. James has been discharged."

He was surprised. "Discharged? But we learned he was attacked too. Why so soon?"

"Well, he asked to be discharged." She explained.

"What about Moyo? When is she likely to be discharged?"

"I'm not certain. The doctor will let you know, but it may be tomorrow. Her bruises are not serious." She said and left.

Lolu kept quiet. Minutes passed, but it felt like hours. The images of Moyo and James lingered in his mind, clouding his thoughts, but he forced himself to focus. He needed to stay composed. He needed to be ready when she woke up.

Another nurse entered the room to attend to the second patient.

Just then, Moyo stirred a little, shifting on the bed. Lolu looked at her, his heart thumping in his chest. This was it— the moment he'd been waiting for!

"Moyo?" Her mother called.

"Yes?"

"How are you feeling?"

Moyo simply nodded, feeling too weak to talk.

The nurse had finished with the patient and came over to Moyo. "How are you feeling?"

Moyo nodded again.

"The doctor will come and check you now." The nurse told her.

When she turned to leave, Lolu came to Moyo. "I have some questions I need answers to." He said, with a cold expression on his face.

The nurse looked back, stopped, and interjected, "Not now, please. She won't be able to answer any questions now. She needs to rest."

"Alright then. We will talk later." Lolu said and stepped back.

Shortly after, he told Moyo's mother and brother that he would have to leave to pick Jerry up from his parents' house.

On the way, he continued thinking, still shocked by what Moyo did. How could she have cheated on him? Men were the ones who usually cheated, and he knew some men who did. He'd had opportunities to cheat with not only Pat, but he refused to, choosing to honor his marital vows and God. Did Moyo know God at all?!

And what would he tell his parents if they asked him questions? He decided he would share only what they needed to know. He was still trying to make sense of the whole situation himself.

He eventually arrived at his parents' house, and when he stepped inside the living room, his parents immediately noticed his tense expression.

"Is everything okay?" His mother asked, concern etched on her face.

He took a deep breath. "Moyo was attacked by some thugs earlier today." He explained carefully. "She's in the hospital now, but she's doing okay."

His mother gasped. "Thugs?! Where?"

"How did this happen?" His father asked.

Lolu kept his response brief, revealing only what was necessary without lying.

He added. "It was unexpected, but she will be okay."

His father frowned. "We should call her. She needs to know we're thinking of her."

"She won't be able to pick up right now." Lolu said.

"Then what about her mother? Does she know? Can we call her?" His mother asked.

"Yes, you can call her."

"I need to go see Moyo tomorrow." His mother added. "Which hospital is she in?"

Lolu hesitated. "That may not be necessary. She'll likely be discharged tomorrow."

Without hesitation, his mother reached for her phone.

As she dialed Moyo's mother, Lolu busied himself gathering Jerry's things while his father helped the boy put on his sandals.

His mother didn't stay on the phone for long. "Moyo's mother confirmed it." She said as she hung up. "She'll be discharged tomorrow."

Lolu's father nodded. "That's good."

A few minutes later, Lolu left with Jerry.

Back at his apartment, he changed Jerry into his pajamas and tucked him into bed. Praying briefly, he turned off the light and quietly left the room, exhaling deeply as he closed the door behind him.

He went inside the kitchen to get something to eat. He was still eating when he received Nancy's call. She said Adesua told her about Moyo, and they began to discuss.

In the bedroom later, he began to search Moyo's closet. He found some documents, the deed to the land, and more incriminating evidence.

He did not sleep until around 2.30am.

****

Moyo asked for her phone and found some missed calls from her office and a client.

Taking a deep breath, she dialed her boss's number.

"Moyo! Where have you been? We've been trying to reach you." He said the moment he answered.

"I'm sorry, sir." She replied. "I was attacked by some thugs and had to be taken to the hospital."

"What?!" He exclaimed. "Are you alright? Which hospital are you in? I'll ask someone to come over right away."

"There's no need for that, sir." She reassured him. "I'm okay. Just a few minor injuries. I hope to be discharged by tomorrow. I'll keep you updated."

Once Alfred and his mother were sure that Moyo was stable and able to have a proper conversation, they sat beside her, their expressions filled with concern.

"Moyo," her mother began gently, "Is it true that you bought a piece of land, and you've started developing it without your husband's knowledge?"

In response, Moyo closed her eyes and pressed her lips together.

"Another question," her mother spoke again, "Is it true that you've been seeing James?"

Moyo's silence made them know she was guilty.

"Why would you do these?"

Alfred shook his head. "We just don't understand. What were you thinking?"

Moyo slowly opened her eyes and let out a weary sigh. "There's nothing between James and me." She insisted. "About the land, I meant to tell Lolu about it, I just hadn't figured out when."

She continued offering explanations, but her mother and Alfred weren't convinced. They firmly pointed out her mistakes, making it clear that she had been completely in the wrong.

Eventually, her mother sighed, reaching for her hand. "You will need to make this right." She said. "This isn't just about Lolu. You have sinned against God, too. You have to start with repentance, and then, you seek forgiveness—from God, and from your husband."

She talked for some minutes more, and then she called Lolu on her phone.

When he answered, his voice was guarded.

Clearing her throat, she began, "Lolu, we've spoken to Moyo at length, and we just wanted to say … we're really sorry for everything. Please, Lolu, forgive her."

There was silence on the other end of the line.

"She made a mistake." Her mother continued, "But she will make amends. I hope you can find it in your heart to let go of the hurt."

Lolu exhaled, the sound heavy through the phone. "I hear you, Mommy." He finally said. "Thank you for calling."

After the call ended, Moyo's mother decided to stay the night with her.

Alfred left to get food for their mother while Moyo's hospital dinner was being served. When he returned, he set the food down, said goodnight, and left.

As they ate, Moyo's mother began speaking again. "Marriage is sacred, Moyo." She said. "Do you remember what the Bible says about it?"

Without waiting for Moyo's response, she continued, quoting some scriptures that spoke of love, commitment, and repentance.

Moyo didn't fully agree with her mother's opinion, but she promised to ask Lolu for forgiveness.

Around 10.30pm, she took her phone and sent James a message to check on him.

He responded quickly, letting her know he was in a hospital and recovering well. He wanted to know how she was, and she said she might be discharged the next day.

He sent another chat.

Can you talk now? Are you alone?

She responded.

Not alone. Talk to you later.

Before she slept, she prayed and asked God to forgive her. Afterward, she pondered her next steps for the project and how to ensure the thugs were arrested.

The next morning, the doctor came to check on her, and by noon, she was discharged.

Her mother wasted no time calling Alfred. "We'll need a ride." She told him. "I'm not sure if Lolu will come."

"Have you asked him?"

"No."

"Well, call him and let me know what he says." Alfred replied. "If he can't come, I'll come."

She dialed Lolu's number, and he answered after a few rings.

"Moyo has been discharged." She told him.

There was a pause. "I won't be able to come." Lolu said eventually. "I'm at work. I also need to pick up Jerry afterward."

She sighed. "Alright, I understand."

****

Shortly after the call, Lolu realized he was greatly upset by the situation. He also hadn't slept well. When he found he couldn't concentrate, he took permission and left the school. He picked Jerry up from the preschool and went home.

****

Alfred arrived at the hospital around 4.30pm, to drive Moyo and their mother home. By 6pm, they arrived at Moyo's house.

Inside the apartment, Lolu sat in the living room with Jerry, who was playing with a toy on the floor. Jerry went to greet them, and Lolu greeted Moyo's mother and brother.

The air was thick with unspoken emotions as Moyo, her mother, and Alfred took their seats.

Jerry came to sit beside his father, swinging his legs, unaware of the threat to his family's peace.

Alfred was the first to speak. "We've spoken to Moyo at length." He said, looking directly at Lolu.

Their mother nodded; her expression was serious yet hopeful.

Alfred took a deep breath. "She knows she was wrong, and she wants to apologize."

Moyo shifted in her seat. Would Lolu even be willing to listen?

Her mother placed a hand on her shoulder and urged softly, "Go ahead and apologize to your husband."

Moyo swallowed hard and took a deep breath. "Lolu, I—"

But before she could continue, Lolu raised his hand to stop her. "No, don't bother." He said, shaking his head. "You did what you wanted to do."

He shifted his gaze to Moyo's mother and Alfred. "Do you both know how she's treated me?" His voice was calm, but the pain beneath it was unmistakable. "Disrespect. Coldness. Indifference. I tried … God knows that I really tried to make things better. I swallowed my pride, I reached out, I was patient, but she rejected every effort."

Moyo wanted to talk but her mother stopped her. "Let him finish." She said.

"And do you know what?" Lolu let out a hollow laugh. "While she was pushing me away, another woman was trying to pull me in. Pat."

Moyo's head snapped up. "Pat?"

Lolu nodded. "Yes. She eventually made her intentions very clear." He exhaled sharply. "I would have told you about her, Moyo. Your support would have meant everything. I needed you, and I knew the right thing was to talk to you about it, but how could I, when you had already shut me out?"

Moyo opened her mouth but changed her mind and closed it.

Lolu continued, his voice laced with frustration. He revealed how Moyo regularly referred to her father's irresponsible behaviors, and how he had been trying his best to prove to her that he loved her and that they were a team, yet she was not satisfied.

As he talked, Moyo's mother realized that the past had affected Moyo more than she had realized. She had thought that Moyo had put the past behind her, but she had not, apparently. "Lord, have mercy!" She said under her breath.

When Lolu mentioned Moyo's comment about her car, Alfred's brows furrowed.

"You actually said that?" Moyo's mother asked, her voice sharp with disbelief and disapproval.

Moyo was angry. "But I apologized to you, Lolu! Why are you bringing it up?"

Before Lolu could respond, Alfred said, "He's bringing it up because you've been hurting him and hurting your marriage! He's bringing it up because of the things he discovered yesterday!"

"Moyo, listen." Her mother began. "I suffered in my marriage. It is true that your father made me go through so much, but even in my pain, I never said such things to him."

She paused, then went on. "Talking about your car was pride, Moyo! Do you not remember what the Bible says? *'What do you have that God hasn't given you? And if everything you have is from God, why boast as though it were not a gift*?'" She quoted from 1Corinthians 4:7.

Then, turning to Lolu, Moyo's mother asked, "Why didn't you tell me any of this earlier? Or at least tell Alfred?"

Lolu sighed, shaking his head. "I didn't want to bother you, Mommy." His voice was quieter now, tired. "There was no reason why we shouldn't have been able to resolve these issues between us. Some of these things shouldn't even be happening in a Christian marriage." He gave a bitter chuckle. "Although, at this point, I'm beginning to doubt her Christianity."

Moyo flinched as if she had been struck, and looked at him with a frown. "You're doubting my Christianity? You think you're better than I?"

Lolu's eyes bore into hers. "It doesn't matter much at this point. You wanted fun, right? And you had it with James. You—"

"You're jumping to conclusions! You haven't even allowed me to talk." Moyo interrupted. "There was nothing physical between us. We were just friends."

Lolu scoffed. "Just friends? You must think I'm a fool." He made a sound. "Well, it doesn't even matter anymore. You made your choices, so, no need to apologize."

Moyo leaned forward. "Lolu, you need to let me talk—"

"There's not much to say. Your chats and pictures with James have said it all. I was in shock at first, but I'm getting over it. God wants me to forgive you, and I will. But please - stay away from me."

He got up abruptly and walked straight to the third room. *I need to clear my head.*

A few moments later, he reappeared, the car key in hand. Without another word, he locked the door to the room, turned and called Jerry. He helped Jerry wear his slippers, took his hand, and walked out of the apartment.

When Moyo's mother and brother started talking to Moyo again, she accused them of taking sides with Lolu. She agreed that she did some things wrong, but she believed she was right in some ways.

At the end, they told her to make sure she apologized to Lolu whenever he returned and assured her that Lolu would eventually calm down.

They prayed with her and shortly after, Alfred left.

Moyo sat in the apartment with her mother, trying to make sense of the whole situation. She did not sleep with James, but how could she expect Lolu to believe her?

When she entered their bedroom and opened her closet, her breath caught. Her clothes were still folded, but not neatly; everything looked disturbed, as if someone had rummaged through them.

Her heart pounded. What happened? She reached out, flipping through her clothes. Had Lolu gone through her things?

Anger bubbled inside her. *What right did he have to search my closet?*

Still fuming, she went to the bathroom for a shower, and by the time she stepped into the living room twenty minutes later, she was ready to vent.

"Mom, can you believe it? Lolu went through my things!" She said.

Her mother, sitting on the sofa, looked up. "Are you sure it was him?"

Moyo scoffed. "Of course! Who else could it be?"

Her mother sighed. "Well, if you have nothing to hide, why does it bother you so much? Only a person with secrets would be concerned about their spouse checking their things."

"No, Mom!" Moyo snapped. "It's not about secrets. He has no right to do that!"

Her mother gave her a long, measured look. "Your marital vows and wedding certificate gave him certain rights, Moyo. And if he's never done this before, then something must have made him start now."

Angry, Moyo returned to the bedroom, walked over to Lolu's side of the closet and pulled it open. Most of his clothes were gone. She knew he must have moved them into the third room.

CHAPTER 10

LOLU HEADED TO his parents' house. He had made up his mind that his parents needed to know at least a little about what was going on.

His mother opened the door for them with a smile. There, it was quiet and peaceful—a sharp contrast to the tension that had filled his own home recently.

His parents were surprised to see them again so soon. "This is a pleasant surprise. How's Moyo? Is she feeling better?"

Lolu hesitated, then took a deep breath. "She's recovering, but … things are not good between us."

His parents exchanged glances.

"What do you mean?" His father asked, leaning forward.

Lolu exhaled. "We're having some serious challenges. There's a lot that's been going on."

His mother frowned. "What happened?"

He hesitated for a moment before finally opening up about the site project, explaining how he had only just discovered the full details yesterday.

His parents listened, their expressions growing more concerned with each passing moment.

Then his father asked, "Moyo … was she alone when she was attacked?"

Lolu didn't want to tell his parents about James. They would be greatly disappointed, and that would not help their relationship with Moyo. As kind as his parents were, they were still human. He also did not plan to mention the issue of Moyo giving her mother lace while giving his mother Ankara, despite her mother's advice. He knew his mother well—she might not say anything, but she would be upset.

"Two men were with her." Lolu answered.

"This is … unbelievable." His mother finally murmured.

Lolu eventually got up to leave with Jerry at 8pm.

On his way home, he called Alfred to find out if the police had contacted him, and Alfred confirmed they had. They had also reached out to Moyo, and the investigation had begun.

When Alfred mentioned that Moyo's car was still at the site, Lolu decided to handle it, after all, Moyo was his wife. He said he would make arrangements to have it towed to Moyo's mechanic the next day.

In his apartment, Moyo and her mother were in the living room.

He greeted his mother-in-law before going to the third room. When he came out shortly after to use the bathroom, Moyo's mother called him.

"I cooked dinner, Lolu." She said with a hopeful tone. "You and Jerry can come eat."

"Thank you, Mom," Lolu replied politely, "but I've already eaten. Jerry may want to eat though."

He asked Jerry if he'd like to eat, and he said yes.

Moyo's mother got up, ushered him to the table, and gave him food.

When Lolu returned from the bathroom, Moyo's mother called him to talk to him again to forgive his wife.

"She doesn't love me." He said. "For example, I discovered that you advised her to give the same lace gift she wanted to give you to my mother. But no, she gave my mother Ankara. It was her money though, so it's okay."

Moyo's mother sighed.

Lolu looked at Moyo, "I won't tell my parents about it, but it clearly reveals the kind of person you are."

Moyo's mother asked, "Are your parents aware of the situation on ground?"

"Yes, I had to tell them today, but I only told them about the building project. Telling them about James would only make matters worse."

"Okay, I understand." Moyo's mother responded.

"I don't understand." Moyo said. "James is just a friend. I didn't sleep with him."

Her mother frowned. "I can't believe that just came out of your mouth."

"That's just how she is. She never apologizes and never sees anything wrong in what she does."

When Moyo started to argue with him, he got up and went to the third room.

****

Later, while in bed, Moyo chatted with James to update him on the situation with Lolu. They also discussed the project and agreed to put it on hold until she could talk to Lolu and the threat from those men was resolved.

On Saturday morning, Moyo's mother and Alfred went to Lolu's parents' house. They were welcomed warmly, but the atmosphere was charged with unease.

Without wasting time, Moyo's mother spoke. "Lolu must have told you about Moyo and the land."

Lolu's parents nodded, their faces serious.

"We were shocked." His mother admitted. "We never expected this from Moyo."

Moyo's mother sighed. "Neither did we. But we have spoken to her. We do not support her actions, and I can assure you that something like this will never happen again."

His parents listened.

Moyo's mother leaned forward. "Please," she said sincerely. "We need your help. Lolu and Moyo … they've had problems, but this shouldn't be the end of their marriage. Can you talk to him and encourage him to forgive her?"

Lolu's mother sighed and looked at her husband.

After a long pause, his father finally spoke. "We will talk to him."

Relieved, Moyo's mother thanked them.

They continued talking, and shortly after, Moyo's mother and Alfred took their leave. Alfred dropped his mother off at Moyo's house before heading home.

Now, all they could do was wait—and pray.

Around 4pm, Lolu told Moyo that her car had been towed to the mechanic's workshop, and she thanked him.

On Sunday morning, Lolu went to church with Jerry. Moyo and her mother were at home and watched Moyo's church service online.

He returned home around 2pm, and with quiet determination, he moved around, gathering some of his and Jerry's personal belongings into a large bag. His mind was made up—he needed to leave for a while. He knew this wasn't right, but he didn't know how he could stay with a woman who cheated on him with her ex, a woman who bought a land, and began to develop it behind his back.

As he zipped up the bag and slung it over his shoulder, he turned to Jerry. "Come on, let's go."

Moyo, who had been lying on the sofa, stiffened at his words. Her head snapped up. "Where are you going with him?"

Her mother raised a hand to stop her, then she asked Lolu, "Where are you going with that bag?"

Lolu adjusted the strap on his shoulder. "To my parents' house."

Moyo asked, "With Jerry?"

"Yes." Lolu replied, his voice firm. "He's my son."

"No, you can't do that!" Moyo shot up to her feet.

She took a step forward, but her mother quickly stepped in front of her to stop her. "Calm down." She said gently. "It's okay."

Then, turning to Lolu, she asked, "When are you coming back?"

Lolu's expression didn't change. "I don't know yet."

Moyo turned to her mother, her voice rising. "Tell him to leave my son!"

Her mother shook her head. "Relax, Moyo. The Lord is in control." Then she turned to Lolu. "Drive safely and give my regards to your parents."

Lolu gave a slight nod. "Thank you, Ma."

"Mom!" Moyo shouted in anger.

Without another word, Lolu turned and walked out with Jerry.

****

When Lolu arrived at his parents' house, they were surprised to see him with the bag.

His mother frowned. "Lolu, what's going on?"

He set the bag down and sighed. "I'd like to stay here with Jerry for a few days until I figure things out."

His mother looked concerned, but before she could say anything, his father spoke. "No." He said firmly.

Lolu looked at him, surprised. "I can't?"

"You're a Christian, Lolu. Running away from your home won't solve anything. You're supposed to stay in your house and work through your problems." His father said. "If you can't resolve it, involve your pastor. Have you spoken to him?"

Lolu sighed. "No, I haven't."

His mother frowned. "Why not?"

He exhaled deeply. "Because Moyo has frustrated every effort I've made to fix our marriage. She -" He was about to say that she cheated on him but stopped.

His parents exchanged a glance.

His father leaned forward. "Talk to your pastor. Let him mediate. But staying here, away from your home, is not the answer."

Lolu shook his head. "I just need a few days to think. That's all."

His parents sighed and shrugged, but didn't push further. Though they didn't agree, they remained silent.

Lolu picked up the bag and carried it into the room he used before he got his own apartment. When he returned to the living room, Jerry was already sitting on his grandmother's lap, enjoying a snack.

Two days later, his phone rang. It was Alfred.

"Lolu, how are you?" Alfred asked.

"I'm fine." Lolu's voice was flat.

"I spoke with Moyo," Alfred said cautiously. "She told me you left the house."

"Yes, I did."

"And that you took Jerry with you."

Lolu didn't hesitate to confirm. "Umm hmm."

Alfred sighed. "Look, I understand that you're hurt. I'm not going to tell you how to feel, but please, reconsider. Think about Jerry. He needs both his parents."

He appealed to Lolu to return to his house, but he said no.

"Well, Moyo wants her son back," Alfred continued. "Let's handle this with care, please. Let Jerry go home. Besides, as Christians, we must always seek to know the will of God."

There was a long silence. Finally, Lolu let out a deep breath. "Yes, you're right." He said quietly. "I'll take him back tomorrow."

"Thank you." Alfred said, relief in his voice. "I appreciate it."

They ended the call.

True to his word, Lolu took Jerry back in the evening of the next day. When he arrived at the apartment and didn't see Moyo's mother, he guessed she had gone back to her house.

Without a word, he walked past Moyo and went to the third bedroom. Grabbing an empty suitcase, he dragged it to their bedroom.

What's he trying to do? Is he leaving me for good? Is this the end of my marriage? How will I cope alone with Jerry? She wondered. This wasn't what she wanted.

She hadn't expected him to take this step. Following him to the room, she stood in the doorway and watched as he began to pack more of his own personal belongings.

"Lolu -" She started hesitantly.

He didn't look at her.

"I admit that I did some things wrong. Let's talk about this, please."

Lolu zipped up his suitcase and turned to face her. "I don't have anything to say, Moyo."

"Okay, I'm sorry."

"Move, please."

She did.

Without another word, he walked past her, suitcase in hand, and left the apartment.

That night, Moyo called his phone, but when he didn't answer, she sent two messages.

Lolu, please ... I'm sorry.

I know I was wrong. Please, come home and let's talk.

But there was no response.

****

On Saturday afternoon, Adesua and Nancy sat beside their husbands, Tade and Luke, across from Lolu. They had all gathered at Adesua and Tade's house, determined to intervene in what was happening in Lolu and Moyo's marriage.

Lolu leaned back in his chair, his face calm but resolute. "I tried so hard to save this marriage." He told them. "But she dismissed every effort."

He reached for his phone, scrolling through messages, photos, and documents before passing it to them. One by one, they examined the evidence. As they read through the conversations between Moyo and James, and saw the pictures, their expressions changed from curiosity to shock.

"This is serious." Adesua murmured, shaking her head. "Nancy and I had no idea these things were going on."

Nancy sighed heavily. "We've talked to Moyo on the phone, and we will be seeing her after church tomorrow. But Lolu… we heard you moved out of the house."

"Yes, I moved out." Lolu confirmed. "I've forgiven her, but I need time away."

Nancy shook her head. "I don't think that's true forgiveness."

Lolu frowned slightly but remained silent.

"Forgiveness doesn't walk away." Nancy continued. "Forgiveness stays and gives another chance."

Lolu let out a small, dry chuckle. "I don't mean any disrespect, but it's easy to say these things when you're not the one constantly being disrespected or cheated on."

Tade spoke, "We understand how you feel, truly, but two wrongs don't make a right. Moving out will do more harm than good."

Luke nodded in agreement. "Space might feel like the right solution now, but distance can create even more cracks in your marriage, and complicate matters."

Lolu sighed. "I get what you're saying, but right now, I still feel I need some time. I just … I need to breathe."

The couples exchanged glances; they could see he was set on his decision.

"Alright." Adesua finally said. "But don't stay away too long. Let's keep praying about this."

Before Lolu left, they joined hands and prayed for him and Moyo, asking God to heal the wounds and restore peace in their marriage.

"If you ever need anything, please don't hesitate to call." Nancy said sincerely as they stood.

Lolu nodded. "Thank you all. I really appreciate it."

When he returned home, his parents called him.

"You've been here for almost a week. When will you go home and resolve things with your wife?"

"I'm still praying."

His father frowned. "How long will it take you to pray and know what God wants you to do?"

"Some other things happened."

"What other things?" His father asked.

Lolu was strongly tempted to tell them about James and how Moyo had been hurting him, but once again, he felt he shouldn't.

"I'd rather keep them between us. That's why I'm still praying." He answered.

His mother sighed. "We don't need to know the details of what's happening between you and Moyo, but if there are deeper issues, that's all the more reason to involve your pastor."

Later that night, as Lolu lay in bed, his parents' words, and Moyo's friends' advice echoed in his mind. He would love to put everything behind him and go back to Moyo.

His thoughts drifted to James, and he recalled how the person who called Moyo's mother had referred to James as Moyo's husband. When he and Alfred visited the site, another man had said the same thing. People must have seen them together often.

Then there was Moyo's secret bank account, the messages he saw on her phone, and the growing distance between them.

Would it even be safe to continue living with her? He wondered. He wanted to go home, but what had changed? Even if he involved the pastor, Moyo wouldn't change unless she truly saw the need to.

He tried to pray for direction, but the weight of his pain and confusion made it hard to hear God.

****

The next day, Sunday, around 5pm, Adesua and Nancy visited Moyo at her home. One look at her, and they could see the exhaustion on her face. Her lips were pressed together as if she was holding back emotions.

After exchanging pleasantries, they wasted no time getting to the point.

"You never told us you bought land, started developing it, or that you've been having dinner with James and visiting his office." Adesua said, her tone sharp with disappointment.

"I was not having an affair with him." Moyo said, her voice barely above a whisper.

"Whether you realize it or not, that was an affair. Maybe not a sexual one, but an affair, nonetheless. You were seeing him behind your husband's back, knowing full well Lolu wouldn't approve." Nancy told her.

"And you knew we wouldn't approve either." Adesua added. "That's why you intentionally hid everything from us."

Moyo took a deep breath.

"We spoke to Lolu. He's hurting, Moyo. Really hurting." Adesua continued. "He feels betrayed."

"And he doesn't feel loved." Nancy added.

"We're not here to judge you, however." Adesua said gently. "But we are here to tell you that if you truly want your marriage at this point, you need to fight for it. And that starts with serious prayer. This isn't just about Lolu, it's about your relationship with God, too."

Moyo nodded slowly.

They talked for some time, encouraged her, and prayed before they left.

Moyo had been in contact with the police, and on Monday, they informed her that three of the thugs had been arrested. They assured her that efforts would be intensified to track down the others.

The following Saturday was Jerry's third birthday. Moyo's mother came over, while Lolu's parents called to pray for him.

In the afternoon, Lolu visited, gave Jerry a gift, prayed for him, and then left.

Later, Adesua called. After wishing Jerry a happy birthday, she invited Moyo to a special event for married couples at her church the next evening.

Moyo had no intention of going, but after lunch the next day, she changed her mind and decided to attend.

As she sat in the church, listening to the pastor's message about God's will for marriage, something changed within her. It was as if a veil had been lifted from her eyes, and for the first time, she saw her actions clearly. She had been so consumed by her insecurities, ambitions, and desires that she failed to recognize how much she was damaging her marriage.

And the reason? Her relationship with God wasn't what it was supposed to be.

The pastor went on. "God's design for marriage isn't about winning arguments or proving points. It's about love, humility, and submission to His will."

As she listened, she let out a deep sigh, knowing she had made many mistakes. She felt ashamed of herself. *God, can you forgive me and help me?*

Pushing her thoughts aside, she listened to the pastor.

And then the pastor said, "God isn't looking at your past mistakes, He's looking at your heart. If you're willing and obedient, you will eat the good of the land. He will help you and restore your joy."

When it was time for prayer, tears slipped down her cheeks as she whispered, "Lord, I see it now. Please … help me."

She had hurt Lolu, yes, but she had also strayed from the will of God.

Later that night, as she lay in bed reflecting on her life, her mind went to James.

Suddenly, she remembered the dream that the General Overseer of her church had shared years ago. He had said that in the dream, she was in a relationship with a man, and they were attacked by a man. When he asked if she was in a relationship, she admitted that she was, and he strongly advised her to end it.

That relationship had been with James. And she had ended it.

But she reconnected with him. And now, just as in the dream, they had been attacked.

As she replayed the events in her mind, a chilling realization gripped her. Things could have been far worse. The thugs had used sticks instead of the machetes they carried. Those men could have killed them.

A deep sense of gratitude filled her. She thanked God for sparing her life and, in that moment, made a firm decision— she would do the right thing. She would stay away from James.

The following Sunday morning, Moyo found herself sitting in the same church, her heart both heavy and hopeful.

At home, she prayed and knew she had to take action.

By Saturday, she had gathered her courage and decided to visit Lolu's parents—with Jerry by her side.

When she arrived, she was greeted with warm but concerned expressions.

She took a deep breath, knelt down, and began, "I'm sorry for everything."

When she stopped talking, Lolu's mother patted the seat beside her. "Come, sit down, Moyo."

She did, and Lolu's parents began to advise her, speaking with the kindness and wisdom of parents who had weathered their own storms. They reminded her of the importance of love, patience, prayer, and humility in a marriage.

In the middle of their conversation, the front door opened, and Lolu walked in.

He paused briefly, his eyes scanning the room. He greeted his parents, then he turned to Jerry and carried him.

Jerry grinned, hugging him. "Daddy!"

Without another glance in Moyo's direction, he strode past them and disappeared into the bedroom he was staying in, shutting the door firmly behind him.

His mother gave Moyo an encouraging nod. "Go and talk to him."

Moyo hesitated, then stood and slowly approached the bedroom. Taking a steadying breath, she turned the knob.

It didn't budge.

She tried again. Nothing.

She turned back, her eyes filled with uncertainty. "He … he's locked the door."

His mother sighed. "Don't worry, he will eventually come around."

His father nodded in agreement. "We will talk to him again."

Moyo nodded. "Thank you."

Shortly after, she prepared to leave with Jerry. Before she stepped out, Lolu's parents gently stopped her.

"Can we visit tomorrow?" Lolu's mother asked kindly. "Just to check up on Jerry?"

Moyo gave a small, grateful smile. "Of course, Mommy. You can see him anytime."

****

As the days passed, Lolu made sure to avoid Moyo. Whenever he needed to pick up more of his things from the apartment, he deliberately chose times when he knew Moyo would be at work. He slipped in and out of the apartment, leaving no room for conversation.

Meanwhile, Moyo found herself drawn more and more to the sermons at Adesua's church. She began attending regularly, sitting quietly in the back, absorbing every word. She was searching, seeking for strength, wisdom, and direction … a way to mend the broken pieces of her marriage, and herself.

The first Monday of December, Adesua gave birth to a baby boy.

Around 6pm, on her way to the hospital to visit them, Moyo was praying with tears in her eyes, asking God to save her marriage, and give her more children.

CHAPTER 11

THAT SAME MONDAY evening, Lolu's phone rang. He glanced at the caller ID and recognized the name: Mr. Goodluck. He had done some photography work for the man twice before, and the jobs had gone smoothly. He picked up the call.

"Hello, sir." Lolu greeted.

"Lolu! How are you?" Mr. Goodluck's voice was warm, as always.

"I'm doing well, sir. And you?"

"Good, good. Look, I've been thinking about you. I've got a business opportunity and wanted to know if you'd be interested."

Lolu frowned slightly, curious. "What kind of opportunity, sir?"

"I need someone reliable to handle my business operations—traveling, taking pictures, managing clients, that sort of thing. From what I've seen of your work, you'd be a great fit."

Lolu was taken aback. "Wow … thank you for thinking of me, sir. Can I ask … what kind of business is it exactly?"

"It's an events management firm." Mr. Goodluck explained. "We organize and capture high-profile events.

Weddings, corporate gatherings, even personal milestones. I'm expanding, and I need someone I can trust to oversee things."

Lolu paused. "This sounds like a big responsibility."

"It is." Mr. Goodluck admitted. "But I believe you're up to it."

Knowing that Mr. Goodluck was a Christian, Lolu told him that he'd like to take a few days to pray and think about it.

Mr. Goodluck agreed. "No problem. That's the right thing to do, but I'd need an answer by Friday. If you're interested, we can meet and go over the details."

"Thank you, sir. I'll pray and get back to you in three days."

"Perfect. I'll be waiting."

After ending the call, Lolu thought about it … traveling? And doing what he loved to do – taking pictures?

He closed his eyes immediately. "Lord, if this is an open door from You, let me know. Speak to me, guide me, and give me clarity about Your will in Jesus' name."

He spent the next three days in prayer, seeking to be certain of God's will. The man said the job would involve traveling … to where exactly?

He also prayed about his marriage and, in the process, realized he hadn't been dedicating enough time to prayer. Juggling his teaching job, photography business; and the weight of his heartache, had left him feeling burdened and tired most times.

He also came to see that, while Moyo had done things that were undeniably wrong, he had his own faults as well.

"Lord, take control, in Jesus' name!"

As he began to pray again on Thursday morning, he knew one thing for certain—he needed to see his pastor. He needed help and guidance. Determined, he decided to go to the church early on Tuesday, before the service started, to speak with the pastor.

By afternoon, he felt assured in his spirit to take the job, but he needed to clarify some things before he could accept.

He called Mr. Goodluck. "Good afternoon, sir," He began.

"Ah, Lolu! How are you?"

After the greetings, Lolu said he would like to come over to see him. "I'd like to meet to discuss the job further. I want to know more about the role."

"Great. Can you come to my office tomorrow?"

"Yes, sir, but I close in the school where I teach around 4pm."

"That's okay. Will 6pm be convenient for you?"

"Yes, sir." Lolu had been to the office before, and he agreed to be there.

When Lolu closed at work, he returned to his parents' house and had a quick shower. He dressed smartly, left, and arrived at the office promptly. The receptionist said he was being expected, and he asked Lolu to proceed to the man's office.

There, Mr. Goodluck welcomed him with a firm handshake. "Good to see you, Lolu. Please have your seat."

"Thank you, sir," Lolu said, taking a seat across the desk.

"So," Mr. Goodluck began, "this job will require a lot of flexibility. You'll need to travel frequently, sometimes on short notice."

"Within the country?"

"Within and outside the country … Ghana, South Africa, UK, US, Canada … as necessary."

Wow! Lolu almost couldn't believe this.

Mr. Goodluck went on. "Your photography skills will be a key part of the role, but you'll also oversee our event logistics. Does that sound like something you can handle?"

"Yes, sir." Lolu said immediately. "I've managed similar responsibilities before."

The man wanted to know the experiences he had, and Lolu told him.

"Good. Now, let's talk numbers." Mr. Goodluck said with a smile.

Lolu listened.

"I need someone excellent for this role, and I'm willing to compensate accordingly." He said and then mentioned the salary per month.

Lolu's eyes widened slightly.

"Does that work for you?"

"That's generous, sir. Thank you." Lolu answered.

"So, are you interested?"

Lolu nodded. "I'm very interested, sir. I'll take the job."

"Fantastic. I'll need a few documents from you—your CV, ID, and a letter of commitment. Can you get those to me by Monday?"

"Yes, sir. I'll deliver them on time."

"Great. Can you start first week of January?"

"Yes, sir." Lolu answered.

"Great. I'll send a detailed schedule before then."

"Okay sir."

"Lolu, I need good performance."

"Yes sir. God will help me; I won't disappoint you, sir."

As they shook hands, Lolu felt a renewed sense of purpose.

At about 5pm the next day, Saturday, Mr. Goodluck called him to say he needed one more document from him, and Lolu promised to bring it on Monday.

"Perfect. Looking forward to having you on the team, Lolu."

"Thank you, sir. I appreciate the opportunity."

Lolu hung up, feeling encouraged, excited, and determined. This was a fresh start—a chance to rebuild and move forward.

As for the document Mr. Goodluck had requested, he would have to go to his apartment the next day to retrieve it. But he preferred to go when Moyo wasn't home. Adesua had mentioned that Moyo had been attending her church, and he recalled her saying that their service usually ended around 2pm. With that in mind, he planned to leave his own church during the announcements, get to the apartment, take what he needed, and leave before Moyo returned.

Shortly after, Lolu's phone rang. He glanced at the screen – it was his maternal uncle calling. He hesitated for a moment before answering. "Hello, sir. Good evening."

After the greetings, his uncle said, "I just got off the phone with your mother. She mentioned you've been having issues with your wife."

Lolu sighed. He should have known his mother wouldn't keep quiet about it. "Yes, sir. We've had some challenges."

"I know your pastor very well. Why didn't you involve him before things got this bad?"

Lolu sighed again before he said, "We were told during our premarital counseling not to involve anyone in our marriage."

"That's not exactly what the Bible says." His uncle corrected. "Yes, couples should first try to resolve their issues privately, but if they can't, they are supposed to involve the church. That's part of the church's responsibility—to help when things get tough."

Lolu was silent for a moment. "Okay, sir. I've already decided to see my pastor on Tuesday."

"That's good. I also heard that your wife has been apologizing. If that's true, you should forgive her and go back home."

"I've forgiven her." Lolu admitted. "I just want to be sure she has truly changed."

"You can't know while you're staying away." His uncle pointed out.

They spoke for a few more minutes before Lolu thanked him and ended the call.

After the call, he thought about his uncle's words. He'd love to return home to his family … he had missed his wife and son. But what if nothing had changed?

Well, he would meet with his pastor on Tuesday. After that, he would talk to Moyo.

On Sunday morning, Lolu went to church as usual, and as planned, he left as soon as the announcements started.

However, when he arrived at the house, he was surprised to see Moyo's vehicle parked in the compound. What happened? Didn't she go to church today?

For a moment, he considered turning back and returning the next day when she would be at work. But after thinking about it for a few seconds, he decided there was no need. He was already here. He would greet her, take what he needed, and leave. Besides, this was also an opportunity to see his son.

Then another thought struck him—what if she hadn't gone to church because she was ill? Or worse, what if Jerry was sick and they needed help?

He would hate to find out later that something was wrong and blame himself for letting his pain get in the way of helping his wife and son.

Making up his mind, he stepped out of his car, locked it, and walked to the building.

At the door, he knocked first to alert her of his arrival, then inserted his key into the lock. He turned it, pushed the door open, and stepped inside.

She was in the living room, lying down on the sofa, with a book in her hand while Jerry was eating.

He saw her lower the book as she looked at him. He saw an emotion flicker on her face, but he wasn't sure if it was a surprise or sadness.

Jerry was clearly surprised and happy as he smiled broadly. "Daddy!"

"Good afternoon." Moyo greeted him.

He was about to respond to her when Jerry ran to him and held him. He carried his son, and then responded to her, "Good afternoon."

He would have loved to ask if she went to church, but he told himself it wasn't his business. At least not now, until things were resolved. And he still needed to know the truth about her relationship with James.

He talked to Jerry, lowered him to the floor, and then he announced, "I need to get a document."

She slowly sat up and watched him as he made his way to their bedroom, his steps measured, his face unreadable.

Telling herself she needed to do something, she got up and followed him to the bedroom.

He was standing by the closet but glanced back when she entered.

She stood by the door. "Lolu, please … can we talk?" Her voice was tentative.

He didn't answer for some seconds and then shrugged as he brought out a file.

"I know I hurt you, and I truly wish I could turn back the clock. I'm sorry. Please forgive me."

"I've told you that I've forgiven you." He said calmly.

"Then come back home."

He didn't respond to that as he continued what he was doing.

"Please."

Silence was her only answer. And that was because he was still thinking of what to say.

Then he asked, "Are you praying for us?"

"Yes."

"Then the Lord is in control."

She kept quiet.

At some point, he moved to leave the room, and she stepped back into the living room to allow him to pass.

He went to Jerry and crouched to his level. He prayed briefly for him and said he loved him.

When he straightened and moved to leave, she stepped forward, wrapped her arms around him, and held him tightly.

He took a deep breath, then said, "Let me go." His tone was not harsh.

"No." She said, her voice trembling. "You need to listen to me first."

"But you've talked! I heard you." He replied, his eyes searching hers for a moment before looking away. "And I said I've forgiven you."

"No, you haven't." She whispered, shaking her head. Tears glistened in her eyes. "Please, sit down."

He hesitated and then sighed. Lowering himself onto the sofa, he leaned back.

She knelt down in front of him, her hands resting lightly on his knees. "I'm so sorry," she said, her voice breaking. "I know I've hurt you deeply. I didn't respect you; I didn't respect our marriage. But I want to make things right. Give me another chance … give our marriage another chance, Lolu."

He took a deep breath but stayed silent.

She could see that he was considering what she was saying. She went on. "I've been going to Adesua's church, and I've learned so much. I'm ready … ready to join you in yours."

He adjusted himself, but didn't talk.

She spoke again. "Let's give our son a chance to be raised by both parents together. You talked several times about raising him for the Lord."

Those words touched him, and he took a deep breath again.

She went on. "Give us a chance to give Jerry one or two siblings that he can play with."

He looked at her with eyes that seemed tired. "You don't love me, Moyo." He said in almost a whisper.

"I do." She said quickly, her voice pleading.

"No, you don't. A woman who truly loves her husband wouldn't treat him the way you treated me."

"I apologize. All the things you've asked for … your hopes for us … I'm ready to do them now. Please, let's save this marriage."

He let out a long sigh, and then said, "Please get up and sit down."

She shook her head. "No, I won't get up until you listen to what I have to say."

"Okay."

She began to speak, sharing everything with him—about James, the land, and everything else she felt needed to be discussed.

She added, "The thugs' case has been charged to court, and it will be coming up in January. But whatever you want me to do is what I'll do. I'm ready to follow your lead."

She paused for a moment, as if considering her next words carefully. "I'm no longer interested in the land. I've thought about it, and I'd prefer that we sell it. I would love for us to buy another one together and build together."

She hoped he would understand that this was her way of wanting to move forward with him, to make decisions together and leave the past behind.

He asked her several questions, and she answered each one.

She explained how her father's behavior had created fear and insecurity in her, but that she had prayed and was now willing to trust God.

She promised to join his church, to respect him, trust him, and be transparent with him moving forward. And she assured him that she was no longer in contact with James.

Then she said, "Tell me you forgive me."

"Okay. Look, you hurt me, Moyo." He said, still in a low voice. "You hurt me, and you hurt our marriage deeply. You made me look like a fool."

She nodded, tears slipping down her cheeks. "I know I did. I see it now. And I'm so sorry. Please forgive me."

He looked at her for a long moment, as if weighing her words. Then he nodded slowly. "I've forgiven you. And I mean it."

"If you mean it, then don't leave." She said, her hands clutching his in a pleading way.

"I will have to. My things are already at my parents' house. But … I'll … I can stay till evening and just go back to my parents' house to sleep."

"And then you'll bring your things back here tomorrow." She finished for him.

He chuckled, then nodded slowly. "So, will you get up and sit down now?"

A small smile broke through her tears. But instead of getting up, she moved closer to him and rested her head on his lap. "I've missed you." She whispered.

He used a hand to rub her back. "I've missed you too."

Then he made his own promises to her … to continue to love her and remain faithful to her.

He also told her all that she needed to know about Pat, and how he had said no to her offers.

As she listened to him, she realized how rare he was. Lolu wasn't just any man; he was a man in a million.

When she raised her head to look at him, he lowered his face and kissed her.

She responded.

"Let's go inside the room." He suggested in a low voice, and she rose to her feet.

Hours later, the clock read 10pm when he finally stood, ready to leave. Moyo and Jerry followed him out to his car, the cool night air wrapping around them.

He kissed her lightly and then gave Jerry a peck on his forehead.

"Drive safely." She told him.

He nodded, his hand briefly grazing her arm before he entered his car. He started his car, and as he pulled away, they waved at him, and he waved back. They stood watching as the car disappeared down the street.

As she walked back inside with Jerry, she felt very happy. God had answered her prayer. He did it again. "Thank You, Jesus." She mouthed.

The next day, Lolu submitted the documents to Mr. Goodluck.

Moyo was able to leave her office early and go to Lolu's parents' house to assist him, and they returned to their apartment. She carried the light items while he carried the heavier ones. Boxes and clothes began to make their way back into the apartment, and soon, they had unloaded the last of his belongings from the car.

They ate the food they brought from his parents' house. Afterward, they began to put his things away and by evening, everything was done.

She told him she would like to decorate the house for Christmas on Saturday, and he said he'd assist her.

Later, as they lay side by side in bed, he told her, "I wanted to tell you something."

She turned her head to meet his gaze, curiosity lighting her face. "What is it?"

"I got a job."

Her eyebrows lifted in surprise. "You did?"

"Yes." He said, a touch of pride in his voice. "It starts in January. A man I know … he wants me to manage his businesses for him. It'll involve traveling and taking pictures."

For a moment, she simply stared at him, processing. "Traveling? To where?"

"To countries."

"Countries? I don't understand. What kind of work exactly?"

He explained to her.

A smile spread across her face as she exclaimed. "Wow!"

"It's a miracle."

"That's amazing. I didn't even know you were looking."

"I wasn't." He admitted, his lips curving into a sheepish grin. "It kind of came out of nowhere. I've taken photographs at his event twice, and he liked them. Last month, he called me and said he needed someone reliable to handle the job for him. When he told me the salary, I almost couldn't believe it."

He told her the salary.

"It feels like a good opportunity." She said.

"Yes, I think so." He said.

She prayed that if this was indeed an open door from God, he would not lose it, and he said Amen.

"I just hope it won't require a lot of traveling, so we can still have enough time together." She said.

"I hope so."

"How well do you know him?" She asked.

"Well, I know him fairly well. And we've been talking since. He's a Christian."

"Oh, that's good."

"I'm supposed to see him on Saturday evening. I'll want us to go together."

"Okay." She reached out, her hand resting lightly on his arm. "I'm happy for you. And I'm glad we … sorted things out before you started. I wouldn't have wanted you to start and then travel out with things the way they were."

He nodded, his gaze softening. "Me too."

She squeezed his arm gently before settling back against the pillow. "I've missed you."

After breakfast on Saturday, she brought out the boxes of Christmas decorations. Rummaging through the boxes, they began to bring out garlands, string lights, and ornaments. Soon, the Christmas tree had been set up, standing proudly in a corner of the room, draped in twinkling lights and ornaments. As some of the lights, ornaments, and garlands were spread out across the living room, their colors brightened the space.

As they worked together, they talked and laughed. When they finished, the room sparkled.

In the evening, they went to Mr. Goodluck's house, and back at home, they sat together on the sofa, holding hands. The only light in the room came from the TV and the twinkling lights. Jerry sat beside Lolu, playing with a toy. The hymn playing on TV was *I have Christmas Joy*.

I have Christmas joy, Christmas cheer!
This year's Christmas draws so near!

Jesus reigns, my Lord, my King!
He saved my soul, His praises ring!
He heard my prayer, my heart is light!
I have Christmas joy, filled with delight!

The melody filled the room.

For a moment, neither of them spoke, content to let the music and the warmth of the moment speak for them.

"I just love this." She said softly, leaning her head against his shoulder.

"What, the decorations?" He asked, glancing down at her.

"No." She said. She raised her head to look at him, a smile playing on her lips. "This. Just being together, with everything feeling … peaceful."

He kissed her forehead. "Yes. Me too."

And for the first time in a long while, it felt like everything was exactly where it was meant to be, and they knew that everything would be alright.

ALSO BY TAIWO IREDELE ODUBIYI
Fiction
*In Love for Us   *Love Fever   *Love on the Pulpit
*Shadows from the Past   *This Time Around   *Oh Baby!
*Tears on My Pillow   *To Love Again   *You Found Me
*My First Love   *With This Ring   *The Forever Kind of Love
*What Changed You?   *Too Much of a Good Thing
*Is it Me You're Looking for?   *Marriage on Fire
*Then Came You   *The One for Me   *Sea of Regrets
*Shipwrecked With You   *Life Goes On   *I'll Take You There
*My Desire   *If You Could See Me Now   *Never Say Never!
*When A Man Loves a Woman   *Christmas to Remember
*Accidentally Yours   *She Who Has a Man   *Comfort and Joy
*Broken Together   *Friends to Forever   *One Day in December
*Made a Way   *To have and to hold

For Children
*Rescued by Victor   *No One is a Nobody
*The Boy Who Stole   *Joe and His Stepmother, Bibi
*Nike & the Stranger   *Billy the Bully   *Greater Tomorrow
*Jonah's First Day of School   *Bimbo Learns a Lesson

Nonfiction
*30 Things Husbands Do That Hurt Their Wives
*30 Things Wives Do That Hurt Their Husbands
*Rape & How to Handle it   *Divine Instructions to live by – 1
*God's Words to Singles   *God's Words to Couples
*God's Words to Older Adults
*Real Answers, Real Quick! (for singles)
*Real Answers, Real Quick! (for couples)
*God's Words to Women in Ministry
*6 Hard Truths About Marriage & How to Handle Them

ABOUT THE AUTHOR

Taiwo Iredele Odubiyi is a pastor and the Executive President of TenderHearts Family Support Initiative, a Non-Governmental Organization, and Pastor Taiwo Odubiyi Ministries. She has a deep and strong passion for relationships and expresses this in ministries - nationally and internationally - to children, teenagers, singles, women and couples. She reaches out to these groups through counseling, seminars and programs such as Tenderheartslink, an online program for Christian singles and couples. Married and blessed with children, she is the host of the YouTube channel – Tenderheartslink!

This is the thirty sixth of her soul-lifting and life-changing novels.

I love hearing from the readers of my books. If this book has blessed you, please send your comments to:
Tel. +1(410)220-5676
Facebook: Pastor Mrs. Taiwo Odubiyi
             Pastor Taiwo Iredele Odubiyi's novels & books
Twitter: @pastortaiwoodub
Instagram: @pastortaiwoiredeleodubiyi

If you have friends and loved ones, then you do have people you should bless with copies of these very interesting and life-changing novels and books!